A Candlelight Ecstasy Romance®

"I REALLY DON'T UNDERSTAND WHAT YOU'RE PROPOSING," IVY SAID WARILY.

"Just a single modeling session," Rich explained.

"No, the other part of your suggestion, to give me lessons on how to attract men." She was blushing, not sure whether to be angry, insulted, or . . . what?

"That's not as outlandish as it sounds," Rick assured her, wondering why on earth he was trying to talk her into it. All he had to do to get another model was pick up the phone. "My profession is making women look fantastic on film. We'd be exchanging services, is all. Strictly business."

"I think you have the wrong idea about me," Ivy said indignantly. "That I'm on some kind of grand manhunt. Actually, I'm very happy with my life just the way it is. I'm certainly not a California swinger."

"Nor any other kind," Rick added, smiling at her.

CANDLELIGHT ECSTASY ROMANCES®

LOVING LESSONS

Barbara Andrews

A CANDLELIGHT ECSTASY ROMANCE®

Published by
Dell Publishing Co., Inc.
1 Dag Hammarskjold Plaza
New York, New York 10017

Dell ® TM 681510, Dell Publishing Co., Inc.

Candlelight Ecstasy Romance®, 1,203,540, is a registered
trademark of Dell Publishing Co., Inc., New York, New York.

ISBN: 0-440-15108-2

Printed in the United States of America

First printing—June 1985

To Skip and Erma Clack, for years of sharing their love of life with others, in and out of classrooms.

To Our Readers:

We have been delighted with your enthusiastic response to Candlelight Ecstasy Romances®, and we thank you for the interest you have shown in this exciting series.

In the upcoming months we will continue to present the distinctive sensuous love stories you have come to expect only from Ecstasy. We look forward to bringing you many more books from your favorite authors and also the very finest work from new authors of contemporary romantic fiction.

As always, we are striving to present the unique, absorbing love stories that you enjoy most—books that are more than ordinary romance. Your suggestions and comments are always welcome. Please write to us at the address below.

Sincerely,

The Editors
Candlelight Romances
1 Dag Hammarskjold Plaza
New York, New York 10017

CHAPTER ONE

"Casey, old boy, we have a problem," Rick said, waiting impatiently for his friend to pick up on the other end of the phone connection.

Wise eyes blinked as the parrot responded with a flutter of brilliant green feathers and a nod of his electric-blue and yellow head, shifting from one gray foot to the other on the wooden perch.

"Jack, this is Rick Winterset." He paused for a minute while his friend greeted him. "I'm fine, but I'm in a bind. I have to leave for Vegas on a job. It could take two or three days, and that's too long to leave Casey alone. Is there any chance you can keep him?"

Frowning, he listened to his friend's involved excuse, knowing that he was going to get another negative answer. No one he knew was willing to take the bird on such short notice. Imagining himself walking into the lobby of the motel, looking like Long John Silver with a parrot perched on his shoulder, he leafed through his address book again. If finding a baby-sitter was as hard as locating a bird-sitter, he was doubly grateful for his unencumbered bachelor lifestyle.

From the large second-floor room, converted into a photography studio, he looked down on his garden, part of the pie-shaped two and a half acres surrounding the Spanish-style California home he'd bought nearly five years ago when, at the age of thirty, he was one of the hottest and highest paid portrait photographers in the Los Angeles area.

Wondering at his increasing reluctance to leave his retreat in the foothills a few miles from the coast, he tried to think of an excuse not to go to Vegas. He certainly didn't need the money, and the days were long past when a temperamental performer like Biffy Rogers could make him jump through hoops for the honor of photographing her. Biffy! It was a name for a bubble-headed teenager, not a woman who'd gone through three marriages, four facelifts, and more comebacks than anyone would be cruel enough to count. He'd been nineteen and still a student at the Art Center College in Los Angeles, learning to draw and paying his way with a camera when a friend of a friend introduced him to Biffy. She'd been his first important client, convincing him that being an artist with a camera was more challenging and lucrative than scrambling for commercial art jobs. His comfortable circumstances and the leisure to paint what he liked were due in no small part to her encouragement.

Owing her so much, he had to go to Vegas. Biffy was booked at a hotel there, and as long as she was convinced that only he could take publicity photos that masked her double chin and tired eyes, he felt obligated to photograph her. There'd be tedious sessions followed by heated arguments over the proofs, retakes, and more disagreements. She'd insist on wearing some white sequined tent that added thirty pounds to her spreading hips and waist, and he'd spend the first day trying to get her into a flattering costume.

Tearing off a section of the orange he'd peeled for Casey, he hand-fed the treat to his parrot, enjoying the nudge of the strong gray bill on his palm. Maybe he was getting old, too. Lately he didn't have any more enthusiasm for getting a leggy young dancer or a bouncy starlet out of her clothes than he did for talking Biffy into wearing something presentable. The only thing that kept him from feeling hopelessly jaded was this retreat, his slice of land covered with full-branched fruit trees, exotic roses that he tended with lavish and loving care, and, in the distance, the changeable color of the hills, varying from season to season and drawing him outside with his paints.

Glancing out the window, he caught a glimpse of a woman moving in the small yard bordering his property in back. A previous owner of his house had sold off most of the original parcel of land, letting a builder construct a string of small one-story homes. Fortunately, in the late 1920s, when the little houses were built, land wasn't allotted by the square inch as it was in later developments. Even from this second-floor window Rick could see only this one house and a small corner of the one west of it.

"Our new neighbor," he said watching a figure in pale pink shorts and a white blouse attacking the patio with a broom. "It's been at least a month or two since she moved in. We really should say hello, Casey."

"Hello, Casey, hello, Casey," the parrot mimicked, repeating these words from his none-too-extensive vocabulary.

Rick frowned more deeply, making a crease of the single line that ran across his tanned forehead, staring out the window and struggling with his conscience. It was a dirty trick, saying "Hello, neighbor," then trying to get her to take care of his parrot for a few days. Glancing at his watch, he considered calling the motel where he had a reservation to ask if they allowed pets in the rooms, then rejected the idea as he considered the size of the cage Casey lived in when it wasn't convenient for Rick to give him the freedom of his perch. Maybe his new neighbor was crazy about animals. She might enjoy a few days with a talking bird, even if Casey's most brilliant comments were "Hot today" and "Damn that cat." Of course, if she had a cat he wouldn't bother asking. The parrot had no affection for predatory felines, not even when he was safely ensconced between the bars of his cage.

Fastening a little chain and weight on Casey's leg to make

sure he wouldn't decide to go for a flight outside, Rick offered the bird a perch on his closed fist, an unnecessary precaution since Casey had never been known to bite an outstretched finger, and walked down to his garden. A low, whitewashed plank fence edged his property, separating his rose garden from the neighbor's yard in back of it. He made his way between a bed of prized white Peace roses and one with his favorite deep red hybrids, appreciating the delicate blooms and their heady scent even though he was in a hurry. He easily got over the fence by sitting on the top board and swinging his legs around, not disturbing Casey's contented perch on his fist. Dusting the seat of his dark slacks with his free hand, he remembered too late that the fence was covered with a dusty coat of whitewash that was hard to brush off. He noisily approached the sliding glass doors beyond the stone patio, calling out a loud "hello." It wouldn't be dark for another hour on this pleasant early summer evening, but he didn't want to scare his potential bird-sitter.

The thrill of owning a private little corner of the world made Ivy enjoy every minute she spent cleaning and tidying her new home. Wearing her oldest shorts and blouse, faded and paint-speckled from her decorating efforts, she started mopping the slate tiles in her workroom, a surprisingly spacious room added to the house by an earlier resident. Now it served her well as a place to design the dolls and doll clothing that had made her dream of a new start in California a reality. Newly decorated with brick-red drapes and black wrought-iron furniture cushioned in bright plaid, there was plenty of room for her worktables, doll cases, sewing machine, and kiln, more space than she'd ever before had to work in. The floor was hardly dusty, but she enjoyed making the slate shine wetly with the sponge mop as she listened to music from the radio. She didn't hear her neighbor's approach.

Squeezing out the mop and turning to do the other side of

12

the room, she caught a sudden glimpse of a dark figure at the patio door. She was so startled to have her solitude invaded that one foot jerked backward and sent the pail of hot water and ammonia cleaner flying. Torn between the spill and the stranger at her door, she didn't know what to do. She had a momentary impression of flapping wings, then a loud rap on the glass summoned her. Water was spreading across the tiles, soaking one sandal-clad foot, and she couldn't have felt more foolish if she'd dumped the pail over her head. Moving a little closer to the door, she was pretty sure she recognized the man as the neighbor who lived so aloofly in the big house in back of hers.

He tapped again, and she moved toward the door, making squishy noises, reluctantly sliding it open a few inches.

"Hi, I'm your neighbor, Rick Winterset." He seemed about to offer his hand through the crack, then remembered the parrot perched on his right fist.

"Hello," she said, startled again by the sudden flutter of green wings.

"I saw the pail tip. I'm sorry we startled you," he said apologetically.

The face framed by the narrow opening did nothing to restore her composure. It was a strong face with a square chin softened only slightly by a single dimple to the right of his mouth. His nose wasn't quite large enough to be called hawklike, but it was prominent, just the kind she'd choose to sculpt for an Indian brave. Above it, the color of his deep-set eyes wasn't totally masked by the fading light, and she was sure they were a luminous shade of hazel that defied color-coding. Brown hair so dark it appeared black from a distance was blown over his forehead by a strong breeze from the not-too-distant Pacific Ocean, and his skin was a mellow tan without the dry, baked look of a sun worshiper.

"It's all right," she managed to mumble.

"May we come in? Casey isn't as ferocious as he likes people to think."

13

"Casey is your parrot's name?" She slid the door open, allowing him to come inside.

How many thieves and rapists tramped through backyards with parrots on their fists? She backed up into the puddle of spilled water and soaked her other foot.

"Did I make you do that?"

He leaned over and righted the pail with his free hand. At least she was sure he'd come over the fence from her neighbor's yard. The seat of his dark slacks was powdery from the decrepit fence. She tried not to notice the muscular swell of his buttocks when he bent.

"Never mind," she said. "It will dry fast. I have all the windows open."

"Some neighbor I am."

He grinned a little sheepishly, not feeling at all in the mood to con her into keeping Casey. She was a mousy little thing, but her legs were something special, lean and strong but nicely padded in all the right places. She was too pale to be a native Californian, but her skin had a healthy color. She could model with those legs, at least for hosiery ads, he thought.

"Do you live in that house?" She gestured limply at the large hacienda-type house that looked lemony yellow in the deepening twilight.

"Yes, and I apologize for not coming over to meet you sooner. Some neighbor I am! Not even a casserole on moving day. Your name is?"

"Oh, I didn't say, did I?" She backed up, embarrassed by the squishing noise her sandals made when she moved. "Ivy Gronsted."

"Ivy, I'm pleased to meet you." He offered his unencumbered left hand, and she touched it awkwardly. "Ivy is an unusual name." Unfortunately it only reminded him of something green and clinging.

"My mother gave all of us names that remind her of sum-

14

mer. The winter lasts so long in Minnesota. My sisters are Violet and Iris."

He supposed she was lucky her mother didn't like daffodils. The real question was: How did Ivy feel about parrots?

"This is Casey," he volunteered, stepping clear of the water that had spread nearly to the sliding doors. "If you'd like to hold him I'll be glad to mop up the water for you."

"Oh, no!" she said quickly. "I mean, I wouldn't dream of having you mop it, but I'd love to hold the parrot. Will he let me?"

"Sure, he loves people."

He transferred the bird to her outstretched finger, long and delicate with a short, nicely shaped nail. To his immense relief the parrot did seem to like her.

"Casey is a cute name."

"I picked it because he struck out, like the baseball player in the poem."

"Oh?" She seemed more interested in the bird than what he had to say, cautiously touching the back of its head where the blue and yellow feathers merged.

"He's a blue-fronted Amazon, captured in Brazil."

She frowned, and he anticipated her reaction.

"Actually, if the natives hadn't sold him they'd have eaten him. He had only a small chance of survival in his native jungle."

"How did you get him?"

"A man I know breeds parrots. He keeps five or seven together and hopes nature will take its course, because it's hard to tell males from females. Casey didn't lay an egg, and he didn't attract a mate. Parrots bond for life, so he was odd man out."

"Oh, poor Casey." She nodded sympathetically, gently touching the bird's back feathers. "He feels powdery."

"Parrots have downy feathers that produce a special cleansing powder. Keeps their feathers glossy. He's really a clean pet. I keep wood chips in the cage—no newspapers to change. All he needs is fresh water, sunflower seeds with a few peanuts and other seeds mixed in, and a bit of fruit, a slice of orange or something. It doesn't take much to keep him happy."

She did seem to like Casey; it made him feel a little less guilty about trying to enlist a stranger as a bird-sitter.

"Does he mind being touched?" She was fascinated.

"Parrots aren't fond of being manhandled, especially not if their wings are held down," he admitted. "But his breed doesn't screech, and he knows a few words."

He tried to make him say "Casey likes Rick," feeling a little foolish when the bird maintained an unbroken silence.

"Casey," Ivy repeated several times, smiling in satisfaction when the bird mimicked her.

"I hate admitting this," he said self-consciously, wondering why this bland girl was pricking his not particularly sensitive conscience so much, "but I came here with an ulterior motive."

The sudden flash of anxiety on her face was too obvious to miss.

"I'm in trouble," he said hastily. "I have to leave right away for a job in Las Vegas, and I can't leave Casey alone. I may be gone as long as three days, but he can stay in his cage."

"Are you asking me to keep him?"

He liked her directness.

"I'm afraid I am. I'll be glad to pay you."

"No."

"You won't keep him?" he asked in disappointment. He'd been pretty sure she would fall for the old bird.

"Oh, sure, he can stay with me. It'll be fun. But I certainly won't accept any money."

"Accept my gratitude, then! I really appreciate it." Maybe because she seemed more interested in the bird than in him, he had a sudden urge to impress her. "I'm a photographer,

16

and Biffy Rogers is one of my clients. I have to take some publicity shots for a new act she's put together."

When Ivy didn't react, he couldn't understand why he felt so deflated.

"You're pretty young. Maybe you've never heard of her," he added lamely, a little embarrassed by his name-dropping. It wasn't at all his style, not after putting up with some of his supposedly glamorous clients.

"Not that young!" She laughed for the first time, a light, tinkling outburst that animated her seemingly plain face. "I'm nearly twenty-nine, but I had no idea Biffy Rogers was still performing."

"She's pretty talented," he said, wondering why he was being so charitable. He thought Biffy had about as much talent as Casey, without the bird's style. At one time she'd been a good imitator, too, but he sincerely wished she'd retire to a dignified profession. She'd make one hell of an agent if she'd start using her real skills and know-how instead of trying to compete with better singers half her age.

"If you're in a hurry, maybe you'd better bring over the cage and things," Ivy suggested mildly.

"Yes, sure."

He hurried home, sprinting when he got over the fence, wondering why this ordinary-looking woman made him feel like a boy who needed a reminder to tuck in his shirt. What the hell, he thought, at least he'd found a bird-sitter.

Sidestepping the spilled water, Ivy stepped out of her sandals and turned on the ceiling lights, studying the delicate creature still perched on her finger. Her artist's eyes saw that calling him green wouldn't do at all. His coloring ranged from the exotic orange circling the pupils of his eyes through a whole spectrum of blues, yellows, bluish-greens, violet-greens, and even reds. She was going to love having him, even though his owner made her terribly uncomfortable. She never felt at ease with men that handsome, and her

17

neighbor had grace and charm to go with his striking good looks.

Knowing that Rick Winterset was way out of her league made her doubly awkward and self-conscious. But then, when had she ever had any luck with men? She wouldn't be in California if she'd been able to fall into an easy, loving relationship with a man as her two younger sisters had. Vi had married a young intern as soon as she'd finished her nurses' training, and Iris had taken a secretarial course so she could afford to marry her high school steady before his graduation as an electrical engineer. Ivy had been a maid of honor five times and a bridesmaid for half the girls she knew in Ramsay, Minnesota. Until her design for the Karol Ann doll had brought unexpectedly large royalties and given her an opportunity to live wherever she liked, she'd fully expected to become the town spinster, Carl and Betty Gronsted's ugly duckling.

Her life was changing. True, she wasn't exactly living in the social hub of Los Angeles, but at least she was away from Ramsay, a town where the minister's unmarried son couldn't sneeze without her mother whipping up a pot of chicken soup for Ivy to deliver. And her sisters and friends were just as bad! A blind date for Ivy became everyone's favorite quest. If she struck out on a date in Aragon, California, and she already had several times with men in her artists' group and the Norwegian Society, she wouldn't be expected to give a play-by-play description of the debacle. Here no well-meaning friend or relative clucked over her bad luck.

She was her own person at last, and she owed it all to Karol Ann. Easily shifting Casey to her other hand, she slowly walked to the specially built cases containing her collection of old dolls and the ones she'd designed herself and sold to a toy manufacturer.

"Casey, meet Karol Ann," she said, not at all self-conscious about talking to a bird who might answer her.

One whole shelf held the different Karol Anns, all with

18

coppery brown hair rooted in vinyl heads and round, rosy cheeks. Each Christmas for the past three years a new series of Karol Ann dolls had been marketed, each wearing a sunbonnet and a folk apron with surprises in the pockets. Karol Ann I had a miniature thimble, thread, and scissors; Karol Ann II had a spoon and a pair of potholders shaped like a cat and a dog. Karol Ann III, not quite as domestic in her Norwegian folk apron, had a tiny pencil, notebook, and reading glasses. Ivy loved home life and was gratified that there were still mothers who wanted their little girls to play with cute, homey dolls. Not even her agent, Sara Goodwin, realized that Ivy had sculpted the original model for Karol Ann from photographs of herself taken at the age of four. Her face, now thin, pale, and more than a little wistful, was nothing like that of her creation.

Rick returned with an awkwardly large cage equipped with food, grit, and water dishes, a variety of perches and toys, and a gilded stand.

"Parrots can't stand drafts. At night he'll sleep in that little box in the cage. I've written everything down, including the name of a vet who treats birds, but he should be fine."

"You'll be gone three days?"

"Probably. Is that a problem?"

"No, I don't have anything special to do until Friday evening." She didn't want him to think she had nothing to do but bird-sit.

"I'll take him off your hands before then. I can't thank you enough for this, Ivy. Sunday evening is a bad time to locate someone to take him."

He wasn't making her feel good by telling her that she was the only person north of L.A. who was available that night. She felt nothing but relief when he left. Mopping dry the stone slates on the workroom floor and enjoying the novelty of having an exotic pet, she preferred to put the parrot's owner out of her mind. She had plans Friday night with a sculptor who belonged to the artists' group she'd joined soon after moving to California. Nate was red-haired, amusing, and talkative, and they'd already gone out for coffee after one of the meetings. The art club was a professional and social organization but not a cooperative marketing group, and she'd already gone out with several members. When Nate asked her to do something on Friday, she'd suggested dinner at her new home; she loved cooking and entertaining.

Casey proved to be an amusing but distracting companion. He was constantly drawing Ivy's attention even though she was under pressure to complete a sample kit with a china head doll and ready-cut clothing to be assembled by the buyer. The little lady was dollhouse-size, just over five inches tall, and designing an easy-to-sew dress demanded all of Ivy's concentration.

In spite of her eagerness to finish this project, she didn't mind Rick's call Wednesday evening.

"Ivy, I really am sorry. This job is more of a hassle than I'd expected. I'll try to take Casey off your hands tomorrow evening or Friday."

Biffy was being more difficult than ever, demanding retake after retake, bursting into tears whenever he tried to suggest changes in her hairstyle, makeup, or costume. His gratitude for the help she'd once given him was being strained to the limit.

"He's no trouble," Ivy assured him, hating it because even on the phone Rick Winterset made her feel timid and inadequate.

"I forgot to tell you; sometimes his seed dish looks full when all it really contains are the empty sunflower husks."

"I'll give him a fresh supply of the seed mix."

"I really appreciate your bird-sitting. When I get back, I'm taking you to my favorite restaurant for a dinner you'll never forget."

What made him suggest something like that? He knew

20

better than to encourage shy little waifs. Lately gratitude was getting him into all kinds of trouble!

"Oh, no, that's really not necessary!" she protested vehemently. Being patronized was much worse than being paid. She'd feel like an orphan out for a treat with the big tycoon. No meal in the world was worth that!

"Well, if you don't want to go . . ."

He was puzzled and a little deflated. The woman made it sound like he'd just invited her to dinner with a lion in the Colosseum.

"I just don't want you to feel obligated. Having Casey here has been fun. It really has."

"Glad to hear it. I'll come for him as soon as possible."

Maybe he'd have a neighborhood gathering and include her. Steaks on the grill would be easy. She could meet a few of his friends, and he'd wipe the slate clean. After this session with Biffy he didn't want to feel obligated to anyone for anything.

"Whenever it's convenient is fine."

Much as she enjoyed the parrot, she wished she'd never met its owner. Now she had to worry about her handsome neighbor taking her on a charity date just to pay for the favor. Another indifferent escort was the last thing she wanted.

Forgetting Rick Winterset was almost impossible with the parrot making the workroom his personal domain. She got a little tired of hearing "Hello, Casey," and "Damn that cat," but she didn't have much luck teaching him a new phrase. When he finally repeated "Crackers, crackers," it was a major triumph.

The doll kit wasn't going well, so she put it aside on Thursday, hoping that by Monday she'd have one of her sudden flashes of inspiration. Most of her best ideas came when she wasn't straining for them. Anyway, she needed time to prepare her Friday evening dinner party for two.

She wasn't polishing windows, scrubbing, dusting, and

vacuuming for Nate Chalmers; he probably wouldn't notice how clean her home was. She did it because it gave her self-confidence to know that everything was in order when she entertained.

Cleaning her newly redecorated rooms went quickly, and she actually enjoyed it. Before the addition of the workroom, the house had had a living room; two bedrooms, one of which was now her office; a kitchen; a bath; and a utility room. The absence of a basement bothered her at first; in Minnesota people dug secure shelters in the earth under their homes, then packed them with "might-need-it-some-day" clutter. Without a garage or cellar she was hard-pressed to store everything in the narrow room with a small furnace, washer, dryer, lawn mower, vacuum, mop, broom, and dozens of other things.

The former owner had carpeted the living room with a thick, pale green woolen rug, too light to be practical but too expensive to discard. Fortunately it looked well with her grandmother's walnut Victorian sofa, reupholstered in a dark pumpkin velvet, and the flowered, two-piece set she'd bought for her first apartment. The one room had to serve as a living and dining room, and it was here that she set the small, square oak table with a white drawn-work linen cloth and tall bayberry candles in spool-turned walnut holders. With her other grandmother's Limoges china, scalloped edges with gold trim, the setting pleased her immensely.

The dinner would begin with fondue, made from a blend of cheeses that included a wedge of Danish, as close as she could find to her favorite Norwegian. She perked it up with a dash of wine and sliced fresh apples at the last minute for dipping.

Not sure whether her specialty, Norwegian beef soup, would be too heavy as a prelude to stuffed flank steak and mushroom sauce, she decided to make it, anyway. Aside from her peppercorn jelly, the soup was her most original recipe. Salad and a blend of wild and white rice would round off the meal. The doll kit had demanded so much attention, she decided not to bake, instead buying some soft potato rolls and an assortment of pastries including some filled with almond paste. A trip to L.A. a few weeks ago had yielded a special prize, twelve bottles of Frydenlund, Norwegian beer that she'd saved for special entertaining.

She was so proud of her peppercorn jelly, made before leaving Minnesota, that she brought a small glass jar to the living room, tying a ribbon under the lid and setting it on the coffee table as a take-home treat for Nate. The translucent apple jelly studded with black peppercorns had the slight tang of white wine and lemon. She'd have to remember to tell him it was marvelous on thin slices of dark bread with a layer of spreadable cream cheese. That and her own special blend of black tea, cinnamon bark, anise, orange petals, cloves, and nutmeg capped the meal.

In a hurry to dress as the time for Nate's arrival approached, she paused to admire her bedroom, the one room in the house that was uniquely hers. Disliking the yellowed knotty pine paneling, she'd painted over it with undercoating and white oil paint, then decorated the walls with rosemaling, or rose-painting, a Norwegian decorative art started in the eighteenth century. Working freehand as many of the early craftsmen had, she'd painted the vine-and-leaf pattern in a soft blue-green, adding stylized blooms in dull red, orange-red, and marigold with accents of black and pale ocher. It took most of her first month in the house to complete the rosemaling, but the bedroom was the delight of her life, old-worldly and brightly cheerful at the same time. Her ultrastark bedroom set, unadorned dark wood with clean lines and a dark blue embroidered spread with thread that had inspired her choice of colors for the rosemaling, added to the charm of the unusual room.

"This is me," she said aloud, deciding not to wear her pale pink shirt dress.

Instead she laid out her long black skirt edged in green

23

and red and the full-sleeved white blouse that went with it. It was her version of a Norwegian folk costume, made to wear at the annual Scandinavian Days Festival in Ramsay. She didn't have a traditional headpiece or jacket, but her blouse was embroidered with eight-petaled red roses and green leaves.

Patting her hair, drawn back into a long ponytail that started low on her head, she decided to go all the way and wear the apron that was an obligatory part of every Norwegian costume. Even brides wore them in many of the regions. Ivy's was crisp white linen with a border of cut-thread work and was held in place by a silver-gilt belt. As a final touch she pinned a brooch on the blouse, close to her throat, a traditional *ornalauv*, a silver ornament with many small discs hanging from and covering it. Dressed this way, she felt ready to play the part of a hostess.

Nate was plumper than she remembered him from the hour or so they'd spent together drinking coffee. His hair, foxy red, didn't quite go with his round face, but his smile was appealing. He handed her a bottle of California wine with a quick apology for being late.

"This place is hard to find. I went past the turnoff and was halfway to Santa Barbara."

"Somehow progress bypassed Aragon," Ivy said, feeling glad that it had. Where else along the coast was there a drugstore in a wooden building with a meeting room for a lodge brotherhood upstairs? "We don't even have a McDonald's."

"Well, this place is cute," Nate said, following her into the living room from the narrow corridor that ran the length of the original house.

"Maybe you'd like to sit here." She gestured nervously at the couch. "The sofa looks comfortable, but it still has the original springs and straw stuffing. The upholsterer thought the shape was too nice to change. I mean, sit anywhere. I have some beer, Norwegian beer. You've probably never

24

heard of Frydenlund. It's very good cold. But the apples for the fondue are turning brown. Maybe we should have that first. Or would they go together? I mean, whatever you like."

"Whatever," he said, sitting back on the couch, laying one booted foot across the faded denim covering his knee.

She was more flustered now than she had been before his arrival, quickly going to the kitchen and taking a platter of sliced apples from the fridge along with a beer. The foamy liquid bubbled over the rim of a tall, fragile glass, and she decided she'd better have one, too. It seemed unfriendly not to drink along with him.

"The apples are just a little brown, not much." She was being too apologetic but couldn't seem to stop herself as she put the tray on the table and hurried back to the kitchen for the beer.

She couldn't cut fresh apples; there was only one left, and it was earmarked as a treat for Casey. Her neighbor hadn't called again. Was he ever going to reclaim his parrot?

"Good beer," Nate said, joining her at the table, dunking a slice of apple in the smooth, warm fondue.

"Would you rather have bread chunks?" she asked.

"No, this is fine."

What had made her think he was talkative? They exhausted the art group and his latest project as topics of conversation before she served the soup. When they started discussing the differences between California and Minnesota weather over the flank steak, Ivy knew that the evening was a flop. He didn't seem to notice her unusual costume, and his fourth beer made him even more quiet. She nibbled at a flaky, but not very flavorful, pastry shaped like a horn-of-plenty and tried to think of something to save the evening.

"Would you like to play Scrabble?" she asked.

"Afraid I don't spell very well."

"I'm keeping a neighbor's parrot," she said desperately, getting up from the table and heading for her workroom. "He's back here."

25

Who could resist jabbering to a bird that might talk back? She snapped on the light, wishing there were some way to tell Nate to go home. He was bored, and it was her fault; men just weren't interested in Ivy Gronsted, not in Minnesota and certainly not here!

Rick made his way through the rose garden, feeling more depleted than he ever had after a job, suspecting that there was more behind his exhaustion than coping with Biffy's hysterics for five days. Her career was on the rocks, and she knew it. She'd called in a favor from an old friend to get a short booking in Vegas, but no matter how good her press releases were, she wouldn't be working the top spots much longer. Rick had done his best, finally persuading her to wear a dark silk tunic over sequined pants that showed off her still-slender legs to good advantage, but the best publicity stills in the world couldn't recreate past triumphs. He'd suggested she go into business as an agent, nurturing young talents and giving them the benefit of her long experience. It was a lucrative profession, and she was a natural promoter, knowing all the right people. She'd hated the idea and had blown up at him. Their parting hadn't been cordial, and it left him feeling weary.

He looked forward to seeing Casey; he'd probably get more sensible conversation from the bird than he had from all the people he saw in Vegas.

The summer days were at their longest, and the sun was just beginning to go down over the Pacific, tinting the sky with swirls of orange and pink. Entranced by the display of color, Rick knocked on the sliding door before noticing that there were two people in the workroom: his neighbor and a chubby man in cowboy clothes. His first thought when Ivy slid open the door was that they were going to a square dance.

"I'm sorry if I'm interrupting," he said quickly. "I'll come back tomorrow."

"Oh, no," Ivy said eagerly. "I'll just get Casey's seed from the utility room. I'm sure you're anxious to take him home."

"Has he been a good boy?" Rick felt a little silly, sounding like an overprotective parent under the gaze of the stranger.

"Fine. Oh, this is Nate Chalmers. Nate, my neighbor, Rick . . ." Her mind went blank, and she felt her cheeks go warm.

"Winterset." Rick offered his hand. "Sorry to intrude."

"Oh, you're not intruding," Nate said heartily. "I have to be going, anyway." He turned to Ivy. "Nice dinner, really nice. Thanks a lot. I'll see you at the next meeting maybe."

"I'll only be a minute," Rick said quickly, picking up on something he didn't like: the guy was using him as an excuse to leave early.

"I've gotta meet a friend," Nate said quickly. "Thanks again, Ivy. I'll see myself out."

She wanted to boot him out, not see him to the door. Couldn't he at least wait until her neighbor left before he took off like a wild goose with buckshot coming at it? Until now her most embarrassing experience had been having Willard Fessing, her date for the junior prom, bribe a friend to take her home. This was worse. Rick's look of sympathy was more humiliating than Nate's departure. It wasn't as if she'd been having fun, either!

She found Casey's food, threw it in a bag along with everything else Rick had provided, and practically hurled it at him.

"I'm really sorry for barging in. I forgot you said you'd be busy this evening," he said.

"You've done me a favor, really," she insisted with false gaiety. "I mean, I was beginning to worry something had happened to you. What would I do with Casey if you didn't come for him?"

"Thank you for keeping him. I really appreciate it," he said with warm sincerity. "You're a good neighbor. I hope I can return the favor someday."

"I enjoyed having him," she insisted. "Casey is really fun.

27

I've even thought about getting a talking bird of my own. I taught him a couple of new words. I hope you don't mind."

"Wonderful! I should buy a parrot-training tape. He's an intelligent bird. I don't spend as much time teaching him as I should."

She watched her neighbor carrying the parrot and cage across the two yards in the fading light, then walked to the living room, blew out the small flame under the fondue pot, and poured the sticky, thickening residue down the garbage disposal.

Poor Casey. She knew exactly how it felt to strike out.

CHAPTER TWO

He planned to water the garden while it was still cool, then, when the sun burned away the mist hovering over the hills, still a lush green from the late spring rains, he'd set up his easel outside and finish painting a landscape. Would he ever exhibit his paintings? A friend who owned a gallery was willing to take a chance on them, but Rick wasn't sure. Without the pressure of needing to sell, he didn't feel ready to expose his work to public scrutiny and criticism. Was he kidding himself in thinking he still had potential as an artist?

Wandering into the studio barefooted and damp from the shower with a small towel wrapped around his hips, he thought again of removing his photographic equipment so he could use the room for painting. The light was better in this second-floor room, and lately he rarely had clients come here. More and more he was taking assignments from ad agencies rather than the lucrative but more wearing contracts with individuals. He'd made some wise investments; the time was approaching when he wouldn't have to earn a living with his camera. Was he hanging in there just to avoid making a commitment to painting?

Feeling far too gloomy for a brilliant California morning, he glanced down at his neighbor's bungalow, regretting again his intrusion the night before. He'd certainly ruined her evening! It was one thing to have a date go sour, but having a stranger witness it was humiliating. Apologizing would only make it worse, but he wished there were some simple way to make it up to Ivy.

Ivy! He didn't know any other girls from Minnesota, but she sure had a strange way of entertaining a man. That costume would be great at a folk festival, but whatever possessed her to wear it last night? Covering legs like hers was a crime against nature, not to mention a bad error in judgment. Well, it was none of his business. After a week of trying to remake Biffy he didn't care if women started wearing chicken-feather suits and big rubber feet.

Dressing in white shorts and a white mesh tank top, he had toast and coffee, then went outside, fully intending to do some weeding before soaking the rose beds. The sweet scent of his garden changed his mind. One thing he could do for his neighbor was cut a bouquet. Her own yard was postage-stamp size, mostly covered by the flagstone patio and shrubs surrounded by crushed gravel, and there was no garden.

Looking over the beds of hybrid teas, he had no difficulty picking out his favorite roses. The Chrysler Imperial plants were heavy with shapely buds and large, dark crimson flowers. They had a rich, spicy scent, at its best in the early morning, and the long, straight stems were ideal for a bouquet. He debated whether to add a few pure white John F. Kennedys and deep pink Tiffanys but decided against a mixture. The deep red of the Chrysler Imperial showed up best against its own dark green foliage. He was more than generous in his cutting, carefully removing the thorns from nearly two dozen vibrant roses in one bed without stripping it of its glory.

The back of Ivy's house looked deserted, so he walked around to the front door. He often jogged down Rimrock Road, but he'd never approached this bungalow from the front. The last occupants had been a reclusive older couple who waved at him over the fence but turned down his invitations to neighborhood gatherings.

She answered the door wearing black shorts and a pink

30

striped blouse that made her look even thinner than he remembered. He had been right about her legs. They were sleek and shapely, sparking a fantasy that made him feel like an old lecher. There was no way he'd complicate his life by trying to get closer to those shapely legs, not when the owner was such a klutzy little innocent.

"I thought you might enjoy a few roses," he said with a trace of awkwardness generated by his lusty imagination.

"They're lovely. Come in. Oh, they're gorgeous!"

Her admiration was so genuine, he felt a little sheepish.

"Put an aspirin in the water and they'll last for days," he advised.

"I've seen them across the fence, but the long-distance view doesn't begin to show how perfect they are."

She brushed one fingertip against a huge red petal with a reverence for beauty that touched him.

"I'm glad you like them." He really was.

"Let me get a vase. I think my grandmother's cut glass would be best."

He followed her into the kitchen, watching with approval as she let the blooms spread out in a large vase that added to the beauty of the bouquet.

"I spend more time in my workroom, but they need an elegant setting, don't you think? Here, hold them for just a minute."

He smiled approval as she removed a linen cloth from the oak table in the living room and spread out one of delicate ivory lace.

"Was that your grandmother's, too?" he asked.

"Different grandmother. They both loved beautiful things. There." She sighed with satisfaction, placing the vase squarely in the middle of the intricate pattern of lace.

"Perfect," he agreed.

She noticed the little ribboned jar, the gift she hadn't given Nate.

31

"Here, take this," she urged him. "It's peppercorn jelly I made before moving here."

"Peppercorn?"

"Apple, really, but the peppery little bits make it great with meat. Or on brown bread with cream cheese." Telling him this was an unpleasant reminder of the previous evening.

"You always keep a jar handy in your living room?" he teased, then regretted saying anything when her face turned somber.

"I hope you don't mind leftover gifts."

"Ivy." He felt exasperated without knowing the reason. "Did you have this handy to give that guy last night?"

"Yes, I thought he'd enjoy a jar to take home."

"You thought wrong." He was too agitated to hold back. "You suffocated the poor guy!"

"I don't know what you mean."

His gift of roses was a lovely surprise, but what had she done to deserve this attack?

"How long have you known—what's his name?"

"Nate. We had coffee after an art group meeting, that's all." She didn't know what to do with her hands, finally clasping them behind her back. "He asked me out," she said defensively.

"So you asked him here for a cozy little dinner instead?" he probed.

"I'm a good cook. I like to entertain."

"That has nothing to do with it. You scared him off! Domestic coziness, home-cooked food, and that apron, Ivy, that apron!"

"It was my grandmother's, too," she said hostilely.

"Fine, but you were a walking advertisement for a good old-fashioned housewife. Old Nate probably sensed a trap the minute he stepped inside."

"I hardly know the man!"

"Then don't spring all that folksy stuff on a first date." He scratched his chin; it always itched when he was agitated.

"I'm a failure with men," she cried out, torn between relief and embarrassment at finally admitting the truth aloud.

"Don't be silly. You're a lovely woman."

It was true, he realized with shock. Her choice of clothing was abominable, her ash-blond hair was a disaster, and her scanty makeup detracted rather than enhanced her plain features. But she had the one thing that counted most: beautiful bone structure. Her cheekbones were high and patrician, her chin firmly chiseled but delicate, her eyes almond-shaped with finely arched brows, and her face an almost perfect oval. His professional eye belatedly realized that she could be stunning, but natural caution made him wish he'd kept his mouth shut. He was through making ugly ducklings look like swans! The week with Biffy had made up his mind.

"Just go, please," she begged.

He really had put his foot in his mouth this time. She was going to cry, and nothing made him more uncomfortable than being responsible for a woman's tears.

"I meant that," he insisted, wanting to defend everything he'd said. "You have fantastic bone structure. I know famous women who'd go through plastic surgery a dozen times if they could end up with a face like yours."

"Oh, sure, eyebrows you can hardly see, and fat cheeks."

She was so defiant that he did a terrible thing. He laughed.

"I'm not a joke!" Her eyes were filling with tears now.

"I'm laughing at your attitude, not your face," he assured her, stepping close and reaching out to stroke her perfectly satisfactory cheek. "If you have fat cheeks, they must be the ones you sit on."

In fact, those were squeezably perfect, but that wasn't something he'd tell a girl like Ivy.

She bit the insides of her cheeks, determined not to lose her temper. She never did. Ivy was the sweet one in the family, agreeable, even docile. Digging her nails into her palms, she wished that this overbearing neighbor would vanish. He made her uncomfortable even when he was being nice, and she couldn't handle his criticism—or his compliments.

"I'd appreciate it if you'd go."

"Make me a cup of coffee first," he insisted, wondering why he didn't back off like any sensible man would.

Glancing at the spectacular bouquet, she knew it would be churlish to refuse, but she almost sputtered her assent. "It's all made. I'll pour some."

Carrying both cups into her workroom, she set his on the small wrought-iron table beside the couch, letting him follow her there. The living room was too cozy and small for this man. She wanted to be in the room where she felt most confident.

"You collect dolls?" he asked, casting around for a safe, neutral topic.

"Yes, for research and inspiration. I'm a doll designer."

"Really?" He walked over to the wall of the specially built glass-fronted cases. "Which ones are yours?"

"All the ones on this shelf." She started to relax. "The Karol Ann series is my big success."

Sliding open the door, she handed him Karol Ann II, her sixteen-inch chubby-cheeked apron girl.

"Cute," he said, examining it with a practiced eye. "You do the whole doll, clothes and all?"

"Yes, I sculpt the original model, then work up the details —costume, hair, and accessories."

"How do you market them?"

"My agent handles the sale. The manufacturer pays me a royalty on every doll sold."

He studied the doll's face with more interest, studying it from all angles.

"Very nicely done," he said, nodding his head in approval.

"She's not terribly original, but children have taken to her."

"Don't do that!" He carefully placed the doll back on the stand.

"What?"

"Don't toss aside a compliment. You put down my opinion when you do."

"I didn't intend to." Damn him, he was shredding what little self-confidence she felt.

He walked with deliberate casualness to the cushioned couch and sat down, slowly sipping his coffee while he wondered what the devil he was getting into. If he had a grain of sense, he'd slug down the coffee and get out of there.

"You have your own kiln, I see."

"Yes, I perform every step right here. My new project is a dollhouse doll with precut clothing. It'll be marketed as a kit. The small size makes it difficult to design an easy-to-sew dress."

He probably wasn't at all interested in dolls, but talking about a familiar subject helped her regain a measure of poise.

"I painted some landscapes for my niece's dollhouse," he said with a laugh. "They taught me a lot, but I thought I'd go crazy working with oils on canvas the size of my thumbnail."

"How old is your niece?" Ivy asked, feeling relieved that their conversation was shifting away from her.

"Nine, and her brother is twelve. They live in Portland. My sister's married to a dentist there."

"Is Portland your home?" Family seemed like a nice, safe topic.

"No, we're native Californians. My great-grandparents came here first. What about yours? All your family from Minnesota?"

"All but one. Both sets of grandparents are Norwegian, but three of them were born in Minnesota."

"Did you go to art school?" He recognized the skill involved in her craft.

"Yes, two years in Chicago." She still wished he'd leave.

"Look," he said, standing to go, "I'm sorry for poking my nose into your business. I shouldn't have said anything about your dinner party."

"You're right, though," she admitted miserably, walking to the sliding glass door, hoping that he'd follow. "I'm just not lucky with men."

"Luck has nothing to do with it. You're scaring them off, Ivy!"

"Oh, thanks a lot." She slid open the door with a bang and stood aside for him to exit.

He closed it again and took hold of her arm, looking around but not seeing what he wanted.

"Come with me."

He propelled her into the bathroom, forcing her to stand in front of the mirror over the sink.

"Look at yourself. Would you try to sell a doll with a ponytail like this?" He flipped up her lank fall of hair, so long that it made a fringe over her forehead when he did it.

Big watery tears flooded her eyes, and she ran away, going through the workroom and across the patio, stymied in her escape by his flaky old fence.

"You've made your point!" she cried angrily when he caught up with her.

"I'm not going to apologize, Ivy. You could be dynamite if you used as much artistry on yourself as you do on your dolls."

"I want to be my own person!"

"Everyone does." He captured her arm and made her look at him. "That doesn't mean you can't make the most of your assets. That's the only difference between you and most of the women I photograph. They take the trouble to learn how to be glamorous."

36

"Men ask me out the way I am." This was true; she probably had some kind of record for one-date encounters.

"Of course they do. You look fragile and in need of protection." Was that why he was having this crazy conversation with her?

"Until they see that I'm a homebody trying to snare them into matrimony," she said bitterly.

"Is that what you want, a husband?"

How could she answer that question? She wanted romance, love, a caring relationship, the kind that blossomed into a lifelong partnership. Rick made her sound so predatory!

"I don't need one," she said stiffly. "I do very well on my own with my dolls."

"There's nothing wrong with admitting you want to get married, Ivy." He dropped his hands to his sides. "For some people it's the way to live."

"But not for you," she said almost inaudibly.

"I like my life the way it is." Now *he* was sounding defensive.

"Good . . . well, thanks for the roses."

"Thanks for the coffee."

She was going to cry; he could see it in the tight squint of her eyes and the clenching of her lips.

A loud horn blast saved him from making a foolish suggestion.

"You have company," Ivy said.

From her yard she could see the end of the drive that curved uphill to circle in front of his house. A leggy blond woman was standing beside a low-slung yellow sports car, waving frantically at Rick.

"Yes . . . well, I'll see you later," he said.

Hopefully it would be much later. His little neighbor was more agitating than he wanted to admit to himself.

He walked rapidly through his rose beds, his thighs strong and tan with hair curling in small whorls down the length of

37

his legs. Ivy was embarrassed to be watching, but she couldn't look away, not even when he greeted the new arrival with a kiss that seemed to last a long time. Well, she'd known from the first instant she'd laid eyes on Rick Winterset that he was out of her league. It was silly to feel so depressed because he had company.

Vivian Cory wanted Rick to take her daughter's formal wedding portrait.

"It will be in all the L.A. papers, darling. You just have to do it!"

"Isn't she a little young to get married?" He felt tired and cynical.

"Nineteen, but when Texas oil comes courting, who counts birthdays?"

"How old is the lucky groom?"

Vivian was too wrapped up in herself to recognize subtle sarcasm.

"Thirty-five."

"Just my age." It would be on his next birthday.

"You're ageless, darling. You will do her portrait, won't you?"

"If she comes here. I can take her Thursday at one o'clock sharp."

Once he'd dreamed of dictating to his wealthy clients. Now that he could, it didn't mean much to him.

"Rick, thank you! I knew you wouldn't disappoint us. Her gown is silk, so you will use your special camera, won't you?" She kissed him again, but with his eyes open, he saw the telltale webbing of lines around her eyes. Vivian looked twenty-five from a distance, but up close she was losing the battle, her skin ruined by too much lolling in the sun and too many late parties. She'd give ten years of her life for a face like Ivy's.

But Ivy didn't know what to do with her potential. What a

waste, killing the fatted calf for a rude nonentity like that Nate.

Gloom hung over his day like the worst of L.A.'s smog, coloring everything he did. He sweated bullets cutting brush on his property, took a long, cleansing sauna followed by a shower as cold as he could get it, then worked on some proofs for a women's socks ad that was due at the end of next week. He wasn't satisfied with them; making sports anklets look attractive seemed beyond his skill. For the first time in weeks his painting didn't tempt him away from other work. In fact, he was strangely reluctant to set up the easel under the big umbrella cemented beside his patio. He was avoiding the backyard.

Dusk found him staring moodily down at the small bungalow, wishing Ivy had enough sense to close her drapes at night. Didn't she know all kinds of unsavory types wandered around, even in the relatively isolated community of Aragon? Nate, for instance: what did she know about him? Just because he belonged to some art group didn't mean it was safe to invite him home.

Damn it, it was none of his business what that kid from Minnesota did. He was only stewing because she was wasting herself; she could be a real beauty.

He went to bed early, lying naked on a sheet that came loose from the mattress as he restlessly turned and twisted. With both Andersen windows cranked open in the corner bedroom, there should have been enough cooling air to keep it comfortable. He hated to sleep with the air conditioning purring away and recycling stale air. Getting up to see if there was a whisper of wind coming through either window, he looked down again on the snug little bungalow. He didn't need a telescope to see that Ivy was working late, standing over a table at the far end of the room.

Without turning on the light he rummaged in the closet for a pair of jeans and some rubber thongs, pulling on the pants without underwear because he thought he'd only be wearing them for a few minutes. Almost as an afterthought he grabbed a shirt from a hanger and slipped into it without buttoning it.

A walk in the garden would relax him enough to sleep. The scent of roses was sweet and fruity in the warm, damp night air, and his weather sense predicted some showers later that night. Maybe that was why he had a slight ache in his right temple.

A feeling he seldom experienced crept over him: loneliness. Rarely did he find living by himself anything but convenient and pleasant, but tonight he felt a sudden compulsion to talk to someone. On impulse he walked to the fence, sitting on the top plank and swinging his legs to the neighboring lawn. A sharp pain pierced the fullness of his buttock, and he groaned aloud, sure that he'd caught a splinter where there was no chance of digging it out himself. He felt the sore spot gingerly, finding a long rip in the denim of his jeans, but apparently he'd been snagged by a nail, not a wooden splinter. Working outside as much as he did in his garden and small orchard, his tetanus shot was up to date. This little poke in the rear was less than he deserved for stalking around in the dark. He'd take it as a timely warning to stay away from Ivy Gronsted's backyard at night. Or any other time.

He was still standing on her side of the fence when light flooded the yard.

"Is someone there?" Her voice was firm and determined as she stepped through the door.

"Someone is," he said gruffly, forgetting his torn pants and walking toward her, slapping at a bug that nailed his neck. "And you're lucky it's me. Never open your door when you hear strange noises!"

He was surprised at how angry he felt.

"I saw you on the fence," she admitted. "I do know enough not to invite a prowler into my house."

"I hope so," he said under his breath.

40

"Why are you here?"

Good question. Why *was* he there?

"I couldn't sleep." The truth slipped out. "I saw your light on."

"Do you want to come in? I'm letting bugs into the house."

He didn't, but he went inside, anyway, at a loss for an excuse not to.

"I finally thought of a way to make tiny sleeves easy to sew. For my doll kit. I couldn't sleep until I cut a trial pattern." She gestured at a cluttered table.

"I do that sometimes, get a good idea and work most of the night."

"On your photography?" The blond woman could've come to his house for that reason.

"No, I find I'm spending less and less time on that. I'm phasing out portrait work, except when an old client corners me."

"Is that what happened today?" She hated herself for asking.

"Yes." He didn't elaborate. "I have a problem on my mind tonight, too."

"Oh?"

"Some shots I took for an ad. Women's athletic socks. They're so thick, the model's legs look like broomsticks. The agency picked her, but they'll blame me for not making the shots glamorous."

"I would think women buy socks for practical reasons."

"The agency doesn't think so."

She was wearing shorts again, and he couldn't keep his eyes from straying to her legs. Maybe, just maybe . . .

"Forget what happened today," Ivy said hesitantly. "I probably gave you the impression that I'm on some kind of grand husband-hunt. Actually I'm very happy with my life the way it is. Moving to California on my own was a tremendous step. I need time to savor my new independence."

41

She'd rehearsed that speech a hundred times in her mind on the off chance that she'd have an opportunity to say it to her neighbor.

"Good," he said absentmindedly.

"Well," she said, not sure whether to offer him a drink or ask him to sit.

"Ivy, we could help each other," he said slowly.

"How?" she asked guardedly, wondering if her explanation had sounded as phony to him as it had to her.

"I need your legs," he said abruptly.

"What?"

"The shots I did for the sock ad are bad. Let me reshoot them using your legs and give the agency a choice."

"Rick, I'm not a model."

"I don't think you know what you are."

She grimaced at him. "Well, anyway, I don't have time."

"A few hours is all I need. You haven't heard the rest of the deal."

"I can't imagine what—"

"Then listen. You have the potential to be a glamorous, exciting woman. I can teach you how. In exchange, you lend me your legs."

"That's crazy!"

"Is it? What do you have to lose?"

He must be crazy, he decided. Where did that idea come from? After working with Biffy he never wanted to give another word of advice to a female, and here he was, suggesting something that could shatter his placid home life.

"Nothing, but—"

"Don't give me your answer now," he interrupted. "Think it over. You can tell me tomorrow morning."

"I really don't understand what you're proposing."

"Just a single modeling session."

"No, the other part of your suggestion, to give me lessons on how to attract men." She was blushing, not sure whether to be angry, insulted, or . . . what?

"That's not as outlandish as it sounds," he said hurriedly, wondering why on earth he was trying to talk her into it. All he had to do to get another model was pick up the phone. "My profession is making women look fantastic on film. We'd be exchanging services, that's all. Strictly business."

She was sensitive; her feelings were easily hurt. He was biting off more than he could chew, so why was he trying to talk her into such a silly deal? Maybe he just couldn't stand to see her assets going to waste.

"I don't know, Rick."

This couldn't be happening. He was the most attractive man she'd ever met, and if he didn't leave her alone, she could easily become infatuated. Playing with fire was nothing compared to the dangers in his suggestion. What made it exciting and off-putting at the same time was that she'd only be a project to him, a challenge like designing a dress for a tiny doll.

"Do you jog?" he asked.

"Yes, three or four times a week early in the morning."

"Good, we'll run tomorrow, and you can give me your answer. Sleep on it. Is seven too early?"

"No, but I still don't think—"

"Just give it some consideration."

And get me off the hook, he wanted to add, stunned by his own rash proposal. He was doing his best to commit himself to an ill-advised scheme to make Ivy Gronsted into a glamorous woman. How could he play with her life that way? She was innocent, unsophisticated. Maybe she was better off as she was. Who was he to tamper with fate?

"Well, all right." She only agreed to think about it.

"Good night, then."

He started to turn, remembered the rip in his pants, and backed toward the door. Feeling the wetness of blood making the cloth stick to his skin, he wondered how he could've forgotten the sharp pain while he talked to her.

She followed him to lock the door, wondering why he was

43

walking backward to the fence. When he was only a dark shadow moving between rose beds, she turned off her outside lights.

Why was Rick so eager to teach her how to catch a husband? Did having a neighbor who was a single woman threaten him and his bachelor life-style? She'd like to believe that, but being honest with herself, she couldn't.

Sinking down on the bright red and green plaid cushions on the wrought-iron couch, she stretched her legs, lifting and studying first one and then the other. She knew they weren't bad, but there'd never been a time when she wouldn't have swapped nice legs for a full bosom and a tiny waist, which both her sisters had. As Bob Fenwick had said two weeks after she'd almost gone all the way with him on the night of Vi's wedding, both her breasts were hardly one good handful. Breaking off with him had been the one time she'd taken the initiative in a long string of rejections.

Lessons! Would Rick expect her to balance books on her head and practice cooing like a mindless bubblehead? Did he intend to have her wear fake zebra skin and blouses that showed her belly button?

She kicked off one sandal and then the other, lying back on the couch and swinging her feet in the air. She was proud of her legs. Pedaling an imaginary bicycle, she decided it had been a dumb idea to entertain Nate wearing a long skirt. What she couldn't tell Rick was that she wanted a man who would love her for herself and that glamorous trappings weren't her style. But then, she wasn't sure that Rick would try to package her like an ad for high-priced perfume. Maybe he really would help her become a more appealing woman. Her own family had told her for years that sometimes she was too honest for her own good, and he'd been right about scaring Nate off with too much cozy domesticity.

Before getting into bed, she carried the vase of roses to

her bedroom, setting them on the polished surface of the dresser. She fell asleep, imagining that each lovely bloom concealed a magic eye that saw her as a golden princess, languishing unseen in a gloomy tower.

CHAPTER THREE

When he arrived, she'd tell him to forget the deal. Wandering barefooted in her pajamas to the sliding glass doors, she stared up at the square bulk of the big house, its symmetry broken only by a wide deck on two sides, added by the sun-loving former owner. The redwood, weathered to a silvery gray, didn't match the old-Spanish style of the house, but it didn't ruin it, either. The house and its appendage existed side by side in reasonable harmony. Could she and its current owner do the same?

Even if her answer to his proposal was no, and, of course, it had to be, she preferred not to deliver it while she was wearing pajamas with pastel umbrellas printed on the rumpled white cotton. Dressing hurriedly, she put on her best red jersey running shorts with a white long-sleeved knit top, pulling the vest that matched the shorts over it. The more layers she wore on top, the less self-conscious she felt, not that she had any intention of running far with her neighbor.

The insistent beep of his alarm did its job, but Rick felt grouchy enough to chew the pillow. He wiggled tentatively, felt a prick of pain where the nail had jabbed him, and wondered if his offer to run with Ivy had been temporary insanity. He hated aimless jogging, thud, thud, thud along the highway. His lean physique owed much to twice-weekly workouts at a health club, but he preferred to get exercise playing tennis or racquetball.

Sitting on the edge of the bed made his rump hurt much

more, and the last thing he wanted to do was hit the road, No, that was the next to last. What he really wished he could do was take back the rash offer he'd made last night. How did he get himself into playing Pygmalion? He wasn't a character in a George Bernard Shaw play, and Ivy certainly wasn't a London flower girl. Although, if memory served him, the original Pygmalion in the Greek myth was a king who fell in love with an ivory statue of Aphrodite. The goddess of love made the statue come alive so Pygmalion could marry it, but Rick couldn't remember if the wedding had been a reward or a punishment. Researching Greek myths had been one of his bright ideas when his career first started to boom. He did a series of photos for a screen star, dressing her like ancient goddesses and heroines. They got a big spread in a men's magazine that brought in more business for him. All of which had nothing to do with the problem waiting for him on the other side of the fence.

He dressed without shaving, putting on baggy gray running pants and a sweat shirt with cut-off sleeves, combing his unruly dark hair with his fingers. If he showed up at her door looking like a bum she certainly wouldn't go for his preposterous suggestion. Stopping in the studio on his way downstairs, he chatted with Casey.

"You got me into this, old boy," he said affectionately. "Next time we'll play pirate, and you can come along on my shoulder."

Better than that, he'd chuck the photography business and concentrate on painting. In fact, when he wrapped up all the jobs he had hanging, he would take a month off, a trial period to see if he could make progress painting full-time. The first thing he'd do would be to convert this room into an art studio. The wedding portrait on Thursday would be his last appointment at home.

This decision made him more cheerful, and he poured some orange juice, sipping it slowly because he had time to kill. Ivy was probably just crawling out of bed, sleepy and cuddly, her mouth stretched into a big yawn. She had a nice mouth, full, pink lips and white, even teeth. It wouldn't take much to get rid of her mousy look: a good haircut, some color highlighting, the right makeup. And clothes. Clothes were the number-one problem. A little simple advice, if she followed it, would transform her into a dynamite woman. Of course, appearance was always the easiest thing for a person to improve. Well, not *always*, he qualified as he remembered Biffy Rogers. It was that naively innocent attitude of Ivy's that scared men away. A man couldn't kiss her without feeling that he was ravishing someone's sweet baby sister. Rick couldn't remember the last time he'd felt guilty for just thinking about taking a woman to bed.

Guilt wasn't all he was feeling. An uncomfortable hardness reminded him how long it'd been since he'd bothered to find a bed partner. Even wearing baggy pants he couldn't walk over to his neighbor's in this condition. Sighing in disgust, he peeled off his clothes in the upstairs bathroom, standing under the needle pricks of a cold shower until he felt like a frozen turkey, skin rough with goose bumps.

"Good morning." He grinned a little self-consciously. "Sorry I'm late."

"Only a few minutes. I always need time to wake up in the morning, too." She smiled shyly. "Would you like some coffee?"

"No, let's run first." Let's get it over with, he meant.

Running made him sweat like a horse. He could use that as an excuse to part company with her right away. He wasn't up to a cozy little breakfast for two. Celibacy didn't agree with him, he decided, not even short stretches of it. His little neighbor was looking much too delectable for his own safety this morning.

"I hope I won't slow you down," she said, wishing he'd ask about his proposal so she could turn him down and get it over with.

"I'm no cannonball on the pavement," he said. He was getting so corny, she should send him packing.

They started down Rimrock Road toward the business district of Aragon, two blocks on Montoya Boulevard lined with small shops and the town's one supermarket. They could have a good run by circling around back to Tyrone Drive, ending up in front of his house. The sea was several miles away, but the breeze was strong, making hair blow back from their faces as they ran into it. He'd been right about her bone structure; it was finely hewn and exquisite, all that any woman could want.

"How often do you run?"

She'd already told him, but he wanted to ask her something, just to prove that he could talk while he ran. Why was he acting like a macho meathead this morning?

"At least three times a week."

Her breath was still strong, she noted with relief, wondering, when he fell behind her a few paces, if her rear was bouncing too much. She slowed so he could move ahead, a mistake because now she could see his whole body thrust into the run, and his movement wasn't remotely related to a wiggle. He moved with a powerful grace that made her throat ache, as it always did when she was confronted with something mysteriously beautiful. Only men didn't want to be that, did they? Maybe her next doll should be a boy; all the rest were girls, and she was ready for a new challenge. She wondered what Rick had looked like at age four or five.

The route they were following was a familiar one, but her mind was taking strange detours. She ran a little harder, wanting this senseless outing to end. The sooner she turned down his absurd proposal, the better.

She was making him compete with her, something he never would've expected. There was more to this little neighbor than he'd anticipated. Through no fault of hers he was feeling angry with her; why did she exist like a little mouse and waste time with losers like Nate? Didn't she know that she could live in the fast lane and be a winner? But maybe that wasn't what she wanted. He certainly didn't . . . anymore. Standing under the shower, he'd made a mental list of all the women he could invite for the weekend. The list was long; he knew a lot of people. There wasn't one he really wanted to see.

He led the way up Tyrone Road, eager for the run to end. Beyond his house the road twisted and turned, not connecting with hers again for nearly two miles. He had no intention of running that far; his shirt was already sticking between his shoulder blades, and he was beyond casual conversation.

"Come in for coffee," he said. It was more an order than an invitation.

She had to get it over with. It would be easier to leave his house after saying no, instead of waiting for him to go home if they went to her place.

"All right."

"Wait here," he said, ushering her into a huge, cool front room and dashing up an iron spiral stairway.

The room was dark, with heavy drapes still drawn over the windows. Turning on a floor lamp, she sat on a straight-backed, dark, wooden chair, one of several scattered at random. The walls were stark white and the floors highly polished dark wood with several charcoal and dove-gray throw rugs accented with touches of burgundy and blue. The leather couch, a deep wine color, seemed half a block long, and most of the chairs were upholstered in gray shades that matched the rugs. The walls were covered with shimmering landscapes, many showing local scenes that she recognized. Thickly textured oil paints captured the luminous play of light on the foothills, always with an animal or human figure to give perspective. She got up to study them more closely.

He quickly sponged his torso, leaving his damp running clothes in a sodden heap on the bathroom floor as he hurried to throw on clean tan shorts and a yellow and white shirt. It was crazy to bring her into the house! Didn't she

50

have any sense at all about avoiding lecherous bachelors? He rubbed the dark bristle on his chin, then scratched it vigorously.

She was perched on the edge of the oversize couch, clasping her knees with both hands, looking ill at ease and tense. Instead of opening the drapes she'd turned on a lamp, and the single dim light seemed hazy in a room where sunlight was fighting to enter through the glass in the door and the gaps between the curtains. Until she saw him and smiled, she reminded him of a little girl sent away to boarding school, nervously waiting to meet the headmistress, expecting the worst. He shook his head to clear away the cobwebs of fanciful imaginings, but even when she stood to meet him, she wore her vulnerability like a cloak of mist. If anyone had ever needed his guidance she did. He knew he couldn't take back his offer.

Following him into the kitchen, she was delighted with the view of her pale buff house with red roof tiles. The real estate agent had assured her that the pear and peach trees still produced fruit, and she'd conscientiously had them sprayed. But it was the lemon tree in the back corner that intrigued her. Imagine having fresh citrus growing in her own yard! Off in the east the rocky hills were patchy with wild blooms, dusty purple and golden orange, and beyond that, a cluster of dark fir trees edged the grassy slopes. Thistle sage and wild poppies were as foreign to her as the foaming crest of waves on the not-too-distant shoreline, and she wanted to soak up every new sensation as it came.

Glancing around the large kitchen as Rick made coffee, she compared it to her mother's cozy little nook with calico curtains and yellow-painted cupboards. All his counters looked like well-scrubbed butcher blocks, and copper-bottom kettles dangled from the ceiling on heavy iron hooks. The floor covering was a brilliant Moroccan pattern, and the walls here were stark-white, too, hung with knife racks and cooking gadgets.

51

"Do you cook much?" she asked, finding the silence between them more than a little unnerving.

"When I have time. Do you like Mexican food?"

"I haven't tried much. Just tacos and enchiladas at fast-food places," she admitted.

"Do you like trying new foods?"

"I love anything new," she said with spontaneous enthusiasm, realizing that this was true. It was the reason she'd come to California, and she was foolish to shy away from any new experiences.

"I'll have to make my burritos with sour cream for you. The authentic recipes use shredded beef, not ground. There were no meat grinders in Mexican villages."

"Just so long as it's not too hot."

"It's a myth that Mexican food has to be as hot as exploding firecrackers. The chili powder and hot peppers are optional."

He put two thick brown mugs on a counter and took sliced whole wheat bagels out of the microwave, setting a squeeze jar of honey beside them. "Breakfast's ready."

They sipped steamy coffee and tried to eat the bagels without letting the honey slide through the holes. Sitting on leather-padded bar stools pushed up to a freestanding counter, they said little and didn't look at each other.

"Thanks for the breakfast," she said, finishing quickly and starting to scoot away.

"Not so fast!" He'd made up his mind; now he had to convince her. "What about our deal?"

"I'm sure you have better things to do than give me lessons," she said, but she wanted to be convinced otherwise.

"I'm not the world's most patient teacher." He didn't expect the warning to scare her off.

"I'm certainly not the fastest learner."

"We'll muddle along, then, won't we?" He risked a small grin.

"If you're sure . . ."

"I don't make offers if I don't intend to follow through." It was a small white lie, he told himself.

"We could try, for just a short time."

"Give me your legs and a month."

"A month? I'm busy. This won't take too much time, will it?"

"No more than you want it to." Did she think he could devote sixteen hours a day to help her catch a man? The idea still made him distinctly uncomfortable. "I would like to do the sock photos this week. Would Thursday morning be okay?"

He could get all his studio work over with in one day.

"Fine. What should I wear?"

"Panty hose and shorts. Only your legs will show. Can you come here around nine?"

"Yes."

"And in the meantime I'll make some appointments for you—my payment for the modeling."

"No! Absolutely not. I have to pay all the expenses myself."

"Top models get a good fee."

"But I'm not one of them. You'll be lucky if I can stand still long enough."

"Move all you like. I have a high-speed camera."

"Until Thursday, then."

Unconsciously frowning, he watched her walk through his garden, climb the fence, and go into her back room. Whatever came of his crazy scheme, the next few weeks weren't going to be dull.

Appointments! Where did he intend to send her? Ivy stewed all morning, wondering if she should tell him that the multilane freeways going into L.A. were almost beyond her driving skill. Her one trip alone, when she'd bought the Norwegian beer, had left her limp and shaky. She never seemed to be in the right lane, and California drivers moved faster than she thought. Even driving in Minneapolis was an ordeal after the leisurely pace in Ramsay.

She pretended to herself that driving was the source of her agitation, at the same time alternatively avoiding the back of her house and sneaking peeks at Rick's house. Like a teenager hungering for a glimpse of her latest crush, Ivy couldn't stop hoping she'd see him for just an instant. Yet the thought of spending minutes or even hours in his company gave her a severe case of butterflies in the stomach. She ruined two tiny doll dresses cut from the new pattern and decided to try again the next day.

Rick didn't keep her in suspense very long. He called before noon Monday and told her to be ready in an hour. Walking up to his drive after vigorously brushing the whitewash dust from her pale pink shirt dress, she'd never felt less ready for anything. She had visions of descending into a mad scientist's dungeon laboratory, there to be transformed into an eerie, otherworldly creation, a strange creature of the night. She nearly turned around and called the whole thing off.

"We were lucky," Rick said. "Sincerely had a cancellation this afternoon."

"Sincerely?"

"Sincerely Valencia. She runs one of the best beauty salons in the L.A. area. I did a layout for a magazine article on her operation a few years ago. That's why you got an appointment so soon."

"How do I get there?"

"Try getting into my car." He walked over to open the door of a brown Mercury station wagon, a practical kind of car that could carry all of his photographic equipment.

She would've expected him to drive a snazzy sports car. Usually his car was out of sight in the garage built into the side of the hill. The drive that swung past the front of his house was mostly used by visitors, and he had a fairly steady stream of those, she'd noticed soon after moving into her home.

"You're driving me?" she asked.

"Of course. I have to see a man at the agency there, anyway."

She enjoyed riding along the ocean, then moving through the confusing urban sprawl with Rick at the wheel, until she remembered something.

"I forgot my checkbook."

"Sincerely is billing me."

"That wasn't part of our agreement."

"You're welcome to pay it if you like."

He wasn't unfriendly, exactly; he just didn't seem to be totally with her. His driving concentration was reassuring, but his absentminded conversation, spotty and noncommittal, made her sure that he regretted their deal. She felt terrible about the whole thing, but it seemed childish to demand that he take her home instead of to the salon. They were driving in a center lane with traffic whipping past on either side, and she really couldn't expect him to turn back now.

The Beauty Boutique in Ramsay had three stations with big round mirrors and buckets overflowing with curlers. The chairs were cushioned with bright blue plastic, and spider plants, sprawling and faded, hung in the front window. Ivy went there twice a year to have her hair trimmed.

Sincerely Valencia's salon was a maze of cubicles with lavender unicorns cavorting on the wallpaper, deep violet chairs and counters, and dove-gray carpeting. Apparently the operators had a choice between uniforms that matched the wallpaper or the upholstery. The owner—her first name really was Sincerely—greeted Rick in person, her thin neck seemingly strained to the bending point by a heavy mass of silver curls, upswept like those of a courtesan in the court of Louis XV. Her age was somewhere between fifty and eighty, but she managed to wear purple velvet on a hot California

55

afternoon without looking totally bizarre. Ivy was amazed to
hear her assure Rick with a Brooklyn accent that her staff
could work miracles. He left her there with a promise to
return.

Some women love to be fussed over, and consider the
expensive pampering of the beautician as a tribute to their
body. Ivy hated it! Being massaged from neck to toes with a
concoction that smelled like coconut oil was the pits, and she
wasn't crazy about having four operators work on her finger-
and toenails at the same time. It made her distinctly nervous
to have several of her long hairs run through a computerlike
device by an operator who muttered over the results.

Most embarrassing was having to ask what they were doing to her. In the beauty parlors she'd visited, the customers
asked for what they wanted. With a special cap on her head
she watched in the mirror as a pale young man with a mass of
coal-black curls carefully pulled strands of hair through the
tiny holes in the cap. Then he covered them with a white
paste that made her eyes smart.

"Highlighting" he called it, and she remembered Rick
using that word.

She was vaguely aware that the dinner hour had passed,
gratefully accepting a snack of vegetable juice and thin,
nutty-tasting wafers from a stern-faced woman in white
who'd earlier weighed and measured Ivy in one of the salon's puce sacks and suggested she gain eight pounds "carefully in the right places."

Wondering whether the beauticians worked all night, she
finally was handed over to the cosmetics department, where
her brows were ruthlessly plucked. Then her lessons began
in earnest. The woman in charge forbade the use of soap,
heavy foundations, and light pink gloss, teaching her how to
darken her brows, shadow and line her lovely blue-gray eyes,
and emphasize her good cheekbones with a touch of dusty
rose blush.

She finally dressed in her own clothes again, assured that

she had a slender neck and nose, long ears better hidden, a posture problem that she could easily correct by remembering to throw back her square, rather thin shoulders, a beautiful, high forehead, and strong arches on her feet.

Her hair had never looked better; in fact, it didn't look like her own pale ash blond. With golden highlighting and bouncy end curls, it made her feel like a different person. She hoped to remember at least half of the advice she'd been given: never use hot rollers or a dryer on her fine hair, use olive oil and a hot towel wrap on the ends of her hair every month, contour her mascara with a wider line, use vitamin A and D ointment on her face at night, work on her carriage, and exercise for body tone. Her brain was reeling; maybe she was high on all the potions, lotions, and magic formulas.

Rick was waiting.

"Very nice," he said. So nice, in fact, that he was a little startled by his own reaction.

"Thank you," she replied lamely.

He certainly didn't sound enthusiastic, but there was something in his gaze—no, she was only imagining things.

"Tomorrow we'll shop for clothes. No more little girls' cottons for you."

He succeeded in making her feel self-conscious about a perfectly nice, basic little shirt dress.

They had dinner at a Chinese restaurant with mostly family trade. Over the egg rolls he said her hair was beautiful, and he approved of her makeup during a dinner for two that included prawns in hot sauce, chicken with pea pods, cashews and mushrooms, and Mongolian beef.

"I'm supposed to gain eight pounds, but not all in one meal," she joked.

"How do you stay so thin?" He had to work hard to keep his stomach flat.

"Sometimes I get too involved in what I'm doing to bother fixing a meal."

57

"I can't get over how different you look." He cracked open a fortune cookie and extracted a thin slip of paper.

"What's your fortune?" she asked.

He kept looking at her. "You really are beautiful, Ivy."

She felt flushed and confused by the warmth of feeling in his voice, but she remembered to say a simple "Thank you."

"Let's see what's in store for me," he said, reading his fortune. " 'Expect exciting changes in your life.' You should've gotten this one. What does yours say?"

" 'Romance is right around the corner.' " She blushed even more. "I guess it's just the standard Chinese restaurant fortune."

"You're not a believer, are you?"

"In Chinese fortunes? I guess not."

"I'm astonished." His smile showed he wasn't. "After my lessons you're going to need a German shepherd to help with crowd control."

"Be serious."

He was, and it worried him more than a little. Now she looked beautiful; with the right clothes, she was going to attract beach bums and chorus boys and aging Romeos, and he wasn't at all sure she could handle them. What the devil had he started? She was even more beautiful than he'd suspected, but how could he change her from a naive little girl into a sophisticated, savvy woman? The awesome responsibility he'd taken upon himself made him gloomy.

"You do look lovely," he conceded. "I know just where we'll do our shopping tomorrow."

She liked Sears and Penney's and other big chains: lots of selection without salesclerks hovering over her, invading the dressing rooms and making unwanted suggestions. She could afford expensive clothes now, thanks to Karol Ann, but shopping for them made her uncomfortable. She was still intimidated by saleswomen in black crepe and single-strand pearls.

He drove to the front of her house, even though it was a

58

long distance by road to his driveway, insisting that he walk her to the door.

"Thank you, Rick. I really appreciate all the time you spent with me today."

"Your lessons are only beginning," he warned gravely. He leaned over, gently brushing her parted lips with his. "Good night, little neighbor," he whispered, intending to leave.

Confused by the way his kiss made her feel, she reached out, touching his waist below the rib cage, startled by the feeling of firm, warm flesh under his thin cotton shirt.

Her shoulders were fragile under his hard palms, and a surge of protectiveness made him draw her close, covering her mouth with his. Her lips had a faint cherry sweetness, soft and yielding under his gentle sampling. Her response caught him off balance, and he had to force himself to back away. The innocent generosity of her kiss made him even more concerned about her welfare. How on earth was he going to teach her not to encourage the wrong man? He knew her warmth wasn't an invitation to spend the night, but how many men would be sensitive enough to suspect or care about her vulnerability?

He went home, not at all happy about having taken Ivy to one of the best beauty salons in the area. Looking glamorous could lead her into real trouble—unless he taught her some lessons in self-defense.

Lying in bed, Ivy wished there was someone she could talk to. She had friends in California: the clerk at the public library, several young women in the Norwegian Society, a few artists who shared her interest in dollmaking, and her older neighbor down the road who'd brought her a blueberry pie the day she'd moved in. But it wasn't the same as having friends she'd known since kindergarten or her own sisters to discuss her problems with. What were her problems? A handsome, appealing man was helping her become more attractive. A friendly kiss between neighbors didn't change anything. He'd kissed the woman who came to his house in a sports car the same way. Probably he was the touching type; a little kiss was just his way of saying hello or good-bye. She was being ridiculous, imagining that there was more to it than that. Worse, she was foolish enough to want more. Rick was doing a Boy Scout act on her; after the fiasco with Nate he felt sorry for her. He couldn't possibly know that his kiss gave her delicious shivers all the way to her toes or that his lips were so warmly inviting, she wanted to cry with happiness.

Her mother always insisted that beds were for sleeping; once her children were bedded down, they stayed there, no radios or reading to lull them off to the Land of Nod. It was a hard habit to break. Ivy lay in wide-eyed agitation, warm in spite of the air conditioning, unaware of the man who prowled his garden under the pale glow of a milky moon.

Until Rick actually came for her in his station wagon, she nurtured a feeble hope that he might forget about shopping. Her wardrobe did need a new look; most of her best clothes had been winter woolens, which she'd given away to friends and relatives when she decided to move to California. She just wasn't sure what her mentor had in mind.

In spite of her misgivings she felt wonderful. The highlights in her hair made her sparkle, and the facial-care routine invigorated her. Putting on her new makeup wasn't at all complicated, and it really did bring out her natural assets. She'd never suspected that simple changes could make her feel so alive and energetic. To celebrate her new look she wore her "California print" dress, a cocoa-brown, full-skirted cotton blend sprinkled with bright yellow and tiny white flowers. It was the only article of clothing she'd purchased since moving.

He came to the front door, glad she was ready to leave. All he'd had time to do that morning was water his roses; until he saw her he'd regretted having to waste time shopping when he could be painting.

60

"You look great!" He'd never complimented a woman more sincerely. "I can't believe how lovely you look."

"Thanks to you." He was making her feel shy again.

"No, and I don't think Sincerely can take all the credit for that glow, either." There was an uncomfortable catch in his throat, so he hurried her out to the car.

"Are we going back to L.A.?"

"No." He started the car. "I know a little shop about twenty minutes from here that has a good selection. My sister wears petite sizes, too. I usually buy her birthday presents there. Nice clothes but not outrageously expensive."

That sounded reassuring. A man didn't usually buy jungle-print sarongs for his sister.

"I need clothes," she said. "I had more for winter than summer, but there wasn't much point in bringing heavy woolens here."

Only five foot two, she did get the best fit from petite sizes, and the store, located in a small shopping mall, specialized in them. Her worries receded as Rick stood aside, watching her select dresses to try on.

"No more pink," he said, taking a pink chiffon dress away from her and handing her a champagne silk with shimmering stripes in the fabric and dolman sleeves.

"I'll probably never wear either of them," she said. "I just thought it'd be fun to try a few dressy dresses. I really need some practical shorts and slacks."

"You'll wear dresses," he said, sounding a little glum.

"This isn't much fun for you."

"No," he admitted. "I'm an impatient shopper. But I've already decided what you should buy."

"Oh?"

"This," he said, handing her a sleek cotton knit with snaps down the side.

The bright marigold shade almost matched the paint she'd used in her rosemaling.

"It's certainly colorful," she said with misgivings.

"And this."

Was she psychic? She'd been expecting something like the cotton chemise he handed her, deep blue with bold zebra stripes.

"I'm not sure that one's for me."

"Try it." He grinned for the first time that morning. "And show me how it looks."

Parading out of the dressing room to show him each garment was embarrassing at first, but the shop wasn't busy, the salespeople didn't hover over her, and Rick's approval was definitely good for her ego. She decided on all three of his selections before trying on red, white, and cucumber-green slacks. Rick rejected the green, saying he wanted to wean her away from pastels. It was the most successful shopping trip she'd ever had, until he handed her a satiny pink camisole with tiny straps and little ruffled panties that matched.

"I'd never wear something like that," she protested.

"Beauty starts next to the skin," he insisted.

"You said no more pastels!"

"You won't want to wear a bra with the knit dress. You'll need a camisole."

The men she knew in Ramsay wouldn't know what to call the flimsy little piece of lingerie. California must be making her a little crazy, standing here and discussing underwear with a man she hardly knew.

"Buy it," he insisted. "I know it's the right size."

She added the two price tags: eighty-eight dollars for a single set of underwear! He looked so insistent, she decided to add it to the pile she was purchasing. She could always return it later.

He offered again to buy the clothes as payment for her modeling but was wise enough to accept her refusal. Insisting on the lingerie had been a mistake, but he didn't want to make a big deal out of it by changing his mind. He could imagine her pert little behind filling the satiny pink panties and the neat mounds of her breasts taut under the slinky fabric. He had to keep reminding himself that she only looked different; underneath her stylish hairdo and makeup she was still naive and vulnerable.

"Do you like this?" She was wearing a huge, floppy-brimmed, white straw hat.

"You look about to take off."

"Oh, it was just a thought." A little deflated, she replaced the hat.

"I love it," he said, walking over to the counter.

"I'm buying my own—" she started to protest.

"Let me have a little fun." He spotted a cluster of yellow and orange silk flowers with a pin attached, indicating to the clerk that he wanted them on the hat.

He paid for the hat with cash and refused a sack, slapping the hat down on Ivy's head.

"Let's have lunch," he said.

They had burgers and milk shakes at a drive-in, but Ivy was too excited to do more than nibble. It wasn't the clothing or her new look or the shopping; everything just seemed more vivid. The clear blue sky was a gift, the warm breeze a caress, the sound of Rick's voice a stimulant. She wanted the day to go on and on, until she realized that he was glancing at his watch every few minutes.

"I'm done," she announced.

"You've hardly eaten."

"Big breakfast, I guess." All she'd had was a cup of coffee.

"You won't gain eight pounds that way."

"I can't afford to. All my new clothes fit perfectly."

"There's always room for another half an inch."

"But I won't get it where I need it," she said self-consciously.

He laughed, but it was a kind chuckle, wholly free of mockery. "You're beautifully proportioned," he said seriously. "Some men prefer women with small breasts."

"Sure." She sucked on the straw protruding from the

creamy pink milk shake, preferring not to discuss her short-comings.

"I'm one of them," he said softly.

"I really am through," she said, handing the wet paper cup to him so he could put it on the tray hooked to his side of the car.

They talked on the way home, but neither of them said anything the least bit personal.

"I'll see you Thursday morning, then?" he asked.

"Yes, of course. Nine o'clock."

"Be careful coming over the fence. I got caught on a nail."

"Have you ever thought of taking it out?"

"You know the saying: 'Good fences make good neighbors.'"

"Good fences don't have nails sticking out," she snapped, surprising herself and him with her sharp retort.

She thanked him profusely for his suggestions and time, but her gratitude didn't make him forget her sudden flash of temper. He couldn't shake off a nagging feeling that some-day they were going to clash on something more important than a rickety old fence. Why had he ever thought she was mousy?

CHAPTER FOUR

The fence was the rambling kind more often seen on horse farms, with flaky white paint and patches of gray, splintery wood. Ivy managed to get over it without snagging her panty hose, but it took several minutes of vigorous brushing to remove the last traces of powdery white from her navy shorts. She lingered for a few minutes in the rose garden, spotting an especially lovely bush in a corner of the garden shaded by trees. Intrigued by pale lavender-pink buds and the open blooms that were almost a pure lavender, she bent to touch one, inhaling deeply but barely detecting the light fragrance. Even if they weren't highly perfumed, the lavender roses were the loveliest she'd ever seen.

She loved being in the rose garden, but it was apprehension as much as appreciation of the flowers that kept her there beyond the nine o'clock appointment time Rick had set for photographing her legs.

From the studio window he watched her admiring his roses and noticed that she seemed especially intrigued by the lavender teas and by a Royal Sunset climber with large apricot blooms climbing up a trellis he'd built his first season after buying the house. She was late, but he couldn't be angry at her for dawdling in the garden. He enjoyed looking at her too much to resent her tardiness. He wished she'd pluck a bright yellow Summer Sunshine to wear behind her ear, but she wasn't the kind of woman who picked her neighbor's flowers.

She knocked on the back door, greeting him with a sheepish smile. "Sorry I'm late. I lost track of time looking at your lavender roses."

"Lady X."

"What?"

"The name of the rose is Lady X."

"I've never seen any like them. They're so lovely."

So was she, he admitted to himself, forcing his eyes away from her slender length and perfectly proportioned legs.

"Let's get to work." His gruffness was directed at himself, not her, but she couldn't know that.

He was a bear behind a camera, she decided as she stood with her feet apart, leaning on a tennis racket, trying to follow orders as she had been for the past two hours.

"This is only the beginning, you know," he said, squinting into a viewfinder, deciding that this series would be the last he'd need.

"The beginning! You've taken a thousand shots!"

"Not quite." He glanced up and frowned. "But I wasn't talking about photographs. I meant, you look great, but improving your appearance is only the smallest part of finding a husband."

"I'm not on a manhunt!" She swung the racket angrily, narrowly missing a tripod, embarrassed that she'd shown her temper.

"If I'm going to help you we have to be honest with each other. You do want to meet someone?"

"Of course, but you make it sound like I have altar fever!"

"Let me put it this way. There's no one special in Minnesota or you wouldn't have left."

"I suppose that's true," she admitted reluctantly.

"And life here would be more pleasant if you had a special friend."

"Friends are always important, but—"

"And if this special friendship blossomed into something

66

more, you're the kind of girl who would prefer marriage to a more casual arrangement?"

"I'm a woman, not a girl!"

"My apologies, but answer the question."

'I'd never feel right just living with someone," she confessed. "I know that makes me old-fashioned, but—"

"Stop!" he interrupted, setting aside his camera. "Never apologize for what you are."

"I'm certainly not a California swinger."

"Nor any other kind." He smiled, the laugh lines by his eyes softening the stern expression he'd worn all morning. "The first problem is to meet the right kind of man, one who's seriously interested in you as a person. That eliminates Nate!"

"It does?" She was surprised by his vehemence.

"Him and any other jerks."

"You really don't have a right to call Nate a—"

"Casey likes Rick, Casey likes Rick."

The parrot fluttered on his perch in a far corner where he'd sat during the photo session.

"Damn that cat!" Casey exclaimed.

"Where did he learn that cat business?" Ivy asked to change the subject.

"I'm guilty, I suppose. The people who used to live in your house had a predatory tomcat. And speaking of predators, you've got to be more careful about whom you go out with."

"There isn't exactly a lineup waiting for the privilege!"

"Well," he said, sounding disgruntled, "I don't think you'll meet anyone worth your time in that art group."

"There are some nice people in it!"

"People, yes, but marriage prospects, no. Artists are too undependable."

"Like you?" She couldn't look directly into his face without remembering his kiss, and just thinking about his lips moving on hers made her senses swim.

67

"Exactly like me."

"You've never cared for one special woman?"

"Of course I have. But not someone who wants to take over my home, fussing over new curtains for the bathroom and lamb chops for dinner. I'm nearly thirty-five, and I've lived alone too long."

"You're just a crusty old bachelor, set in your ways?"

"Something like that," he said crossly, "but we're talking about your future, not mine."

"How many lessons do you think I'll need to get a husband?"

"Lesson number one: don't be flip. You're not very good at it."

"Rick, I may look better—"

"You do, definitely."

"But I'm still the same person. I can't be someone I'm not!"

"Ivy," he said, "let's take it one step at a time. I think what you need is a practice date."

"Practice?"

"With me. It will be a trial run. We'll go through the whole first-date routine."

"Why?"

"I can't sit here and tell you everything you need to know. Think of it as educational role-playing."

"You'll play the role of a prospective husband?"

"No man is a prospective husband on the first date."

"Then what—"

"Did you fire a perfect doll's head the first time you tried?"

"Of course not. It took me months to master all the techniques."

"Exactly. You made practice models."

The connection between finding a husband and making a doll's head eluded her, but the consequences of spending an evening with Rick didn't. If it was a good idea, why did she have a knot in her stomach? Common sense told her she couldn't pretend with him, but she was willing to spend time with him on any terms. That was her biggest problem.

"I've been invited to a party Saturday evening. You can come with me."

"But I haven't been invited."

"The host and hostess expect me to bring someone," he said impatiently.

"If I don't go with you who will?"

"That doesn't matter."

It did to her.

"I'll come for you at eight. It's a beach party, but that doesn't mean jeans and T-shirt. Wear the orange knit dress."

"The marigold one?"

"That's right. And sandals. Heels are too awkward in the sand. And you can wear the floppy straw hat if you like."

"I have your permission?"

He ignored her sarcasm.

"Gretel and Paul Ramon are giving the party. He's a realtor. He sold me this house, as a matter of fact. She makes enameled jewelry. Sells it all over the country."

"Will I need a bathing suit?"

"If there's any swimming it'll be skinny-dipping, but we'll be gone by then."

"You mean we're only making an appearance at the party?" She had to remember she was going with him for practice, not because he wanted to spend the evening with her.

"Something like that. I have another appointment this afternoon. A wedding portrait." He sounded unhappy about it. "Come on, I'll walk you to the door."

He'd never believed the devil made anyone do anything, but for no reason at all he took a swing at her rear, connecting with a soft whack, knowing he deserved the anger that flashed across her face.

"Just part of your lessons," he muttered more to himself than to her, wondering if his subconscious was trying to warn her against him.

"What part?" she demanded.

"Be wary of men who get fresh."

"I know that already."

Her Saturday started as a calm, ordinary day, but long before Rick was due, she was teetering on the edge of panic, torn between deep dread and wild excitement. One minute she pictured him as a staid schoolmaster, impatiently rapping a ruler on the edge of the desk when she didn't know her lesson. The next moment her fantasy took her to a palm-studded beach where he waited at the edge of the water, strong arms outstretched, inviting her to embrace his golden torso.

"Dumb, dumb, dumb!" she said, deciding she should get a parrot of her own as an excuse to talk to herself. Maybe she could buy a female and give poor Casey another shot at fatherhood. But Rick said it was almost impossible to tell the boys and girls apart until an egg showed up. "Sorry, Casey. Poor, poor Casey. Poor, poor Ivy," she lamented.

Not believing for one minute that anything would come of her neighbor's scheme to make her a new person, she indulged in a short bout of self-pity. He certainly wasn't interested in her as a woman! Would he stay for the skinny-dipping that would inevitably occur at his friends' party if she wasn't his date? Not for a moment did she doubt that he would.

Rick came to her door wearing a navy linen blazer with a white silk shirt open at the throat and white slacks that hugged his muscular thighs. Deep-set hazel eyes studied her for a long moment. He'd gotten a haircut—hairstyling better described it—and the thick mahogany waves were combed to one side.

"You look," he started to say *luscious*, "elegant. Like the cover of *Vogue.*"

She knew he was exaggerating, but she wasn't immune to his praise.

"Thank you," she said softly.

"It's a long drive. I guess we should go." He was sorry he hadn't thought to bring a small bouquet of roses to replace the silk flowers on her hat.

"This hat will probably blow into the ocean," she joked.

"Just so long as it doesn't carry you with it."

He was uncomfortable, knowing how much he'd like to see her standing in the foaming surf, the bright dress soaking wet and clinging to every delicious curve of her body. Or better still, lying naked in the sand where the water could wash over her creamy flesh. And he was committed to helping her steer clear of Californians on the make! Why the hell hadn't she stayed in Minnesota and married some upright citizen who served on the school board and got his kicks out of winning at pinochle?

She locked the door, remembering to leave a light glowing, then smiled tentatively and tucked her small hand into the crook of his arm, faking a poise that didn't come naturally. Knowing that she didn't belong with this lithe, graceful man, so confident of his place in the world, diminished her small store of self-confidence, making her wish she was going out with a comfortable, ordinary man. Even Nate was easier to cope with than the virile man at her side.

"Don't be so quiet," he said as they drove northward along the coast.

"I don't have anything to say."

"This is a first date, remember. You have to think of something to say."

"I could ask you about your family."

"Fine, except you already have."

"But if this were our first date I wouldn't have."

"True, but let's assume we've exhausted that subject. What next?"

"Do you enjoy your work?"

"That's always a good opening." But it wasn't a subject he wanted to discuss.

"Well, do you?" she insisted, relieved to find something to say.

"Photography? Not as much as I used to."

"Why not?"

"Another pointer, Ivy. If you get an evasive answer drop the subject."

"Was that an evasive answer?"

"Of course it was."

"You don't need to snap!"

"I wasn't." He spoke very softly. "Tell me, how did you get into the doll-making business?"

"I thought men liked to talk about themselves."

"Some do. I'm really interested in your dolls."

"Most men think it's more a hobby than a profession."

"I don't."

"Thank you. There's not much of a story, though. I'd made quite a few to sell locally. A dealer took some to a doll show, and my agent saw them. She arranged all my sales to manufacturers."

He turned on the radio louder than she liked it.

"Do you like hard rock?" she asked.

"No, not really." He changed the station, found more of the same, then turned it off.

"What kind of music do you like?" she tried again.

He laughed without intending to hurt her feelings.

"You said people are supposed to talk on a first date," she reminded him.

"Yes, I'm sorry, Ivy. I just have things on my mind tonight. I should've picked some roses for Gretel. The red in the Chrysler Imperials is the best I've ever had."

"Do you know the names of all your roses?"

"Yes, since I bought and planted them myself."

"Why don't you paint roses? You love them so much."

"Ivy, you're a very uncomfortable first date."

72

"I'm only making conversation."

"You have a knack for zeroing in on personal sore spots."

"I don't know what you mean."

"I'm fed up with photography, chasing after wealthy clients and trying to make them look like goddesses."

"Are all your clients women?"

"Most. This is the age of specialization."

"I don't see what that has to do with painting roses."

"I'd like to paint as a career." He felt a little foolish admitting it; the world was full of frustrated would-be artists, and he'd be giving up a lucrative living to join them.

"But if you don't have enough talent to recreate the beauty of a rose, you're not sure you're good enough?"

His deep sigh was answer enough.

"Have you ever tried painting roses?" she asked.

"No. Drop it, Ivy."

"Landscapes are farther away and less demanding?"

He didn't answer. She was flunking her lesson on small talk.

"It's just the way I am," she said miserably. "I never intend to pry."

"You weren't prying. I shouldn't be so oversensitive." He wondered how long they'd have to stay at the party.

"Can we start over?" she asked. "What about the theater? Do you like to go to plays?"

"Very much." He smiled in spite of his misgivings, and they passed a few minutes pleasantly talking about their favorites.

The Ramons were the only people Ivy had ever met who, at least at first sight, fit her preconceived picture of California swingers. Gretel was sun-bronzed and draped in colorful, clanging jewelry; Paul greeted his guests in a flowing white robe tied with a length of braided electrical wire. Rick told her in front of them that they were hippies who'd sold out, accidently getting rich when a huge corporation wanted the little mortgaged farm they'd bought to start a commune.

Both of them laughed loudly, and Ivy wasn't sure whether Rick was making it up. In fact, she felt like a visitor on an alien planet, not at all comfortable with the gushing, back-slapping crowd. Three different strangers threw their arms around her, kissed her, and said how glad they were to see her again.

Something green was being ladled into waxy paper cups from an old copper washtub. She accepted a full cup, taking a small sip and trying to decide if it really was spinach-flavored vodka. Hoping a few ounces wouldn't hurt the big healthy tree in a planter, she secretively deposited the remainder of hers there.

Most of the guests were outside, sprawled out in aluminum and nylon recliners and chairs or knocking a volleyball back and forth over a tattered net.

There didn't seem to be any similarity of age, profession, or social status linking the guests, and Rick only knew a few of them.

"Who are all these people?" Ivy asked, holding on to her hat as she followed Rick to the water's edge.

"Mostly prospective clients and a few old ones like me. Paul's selling apartments in a new condo."

"This is how he sells real estate?"

"This is how he sells potential buyers on the wild, free life in sunny California."

"Don't these people already live in California?"

"Sure." He sounded amused. "But Paul's selling more than condos. He's selling a life-style."

"Were you putting me on about the hippie part?"

"Yes and no. They were into some wild things until Paul, Senior, had a heart attack and retired to Florida on his bank stock. Junior took over his father's real estate firm."

"I've always wondered what happened to all the hippies."

"Gretel always had too much common sense to let Paul get into the heavy stuff."

"Drugs, you mean?"

74

"Among other things. Would you like a decent drink?" He was holding a glass of clean amber liquid.

"Do you suppose they have a cola?"

"I'll see. I'll put your hat in the car before it blows away. Wait here."

The volleyball game broke up, and Ivy gave up on her sandals, taking them off to shake out the sand. She was too shy to join one of the laughing, bantering groups of strangers, so she sat by herself in a webbed chair after replacing her shoes. Was she the only one there who noticed the spectacular streaks of color left by the sinking sun over the ocean?

"Hello." A young man in white jeans and a T-shirt that said REDFIELD ROCKETS squatted beside her chair. "I'm Josh McNally."

"Ivy Gronsted. This beach is magnificent. Have you been here before?"

"Sure. Paul's my uncle, but I don't usually come to his beach parties. They're more for his clients. Are you going to buy a condo from him?"

"Oh, no." She giggled a little self-consciously, wondering if this nice-looking blond man would've talked to her before her trip to Sincerely's salon. "I just moved here. I bought a house."

"Really? Where are you from?" He sat on the sandy ground, crossing his legs Indian-style and looking up at her, reminding her a little of an actor who'd played a Viking in an old movie.

"Minnesota. Ramsay, Minnesota."

"You came here all by yourself?"

"Yes."

"Did Paul sell you your house?"

"No, it's just a little bungalow in Aragon. He did sell my neighbor's house to him, though."

She was enjoying Josh's attentiveness, not finding it at all difficult to talk to him.

75

"Here's your drink," Rick said, standing behind her and handing it over her shoulder.

"This is my neighbor," Ivy said, turning and starting to introduce the two men.

"We've met," Rick said dryly.

"Well, nice meeting you, Ivy." Josh got up and ambled toward the house.

"I was practicing my small talk," she said.

"Well, you can practice with me." He sat on the sand by her feet, sipping his drink and looking so glum, he discouraged any attempt at conversation.

"Seems a waste," she mused more to herself than to him. "All this shoreline and no one even wading in it."

"Well, my business is done. We might as well leave."

"We just got here."

"I only came to turn Paul down in person on a job he wants me to do, some shots for a brochure."

Someone had brought a tape player outside, and several couples were dancing to soft rock music, making the planks of the wooden deck vibrate as Ivy walked across it with him.

"Dance with me, Rick," she said impulsively.

He stopped but didn't say anything.

"Believe it or not, you don't need to teach me how to dance." She made a few tentative gyrations and moved her arms in rhythm with the music.

He looked reluctant but took her hand and moved to an uncrowded corner of the deck. Before they could start, the music changed to a slow, dreamy number. Ivy thought for a moment that he wasn't going to dance, then one hand slid around her waist while the other took her hand.

He led her in a simple step, a natural sense of rhythm making him a smooth dancer. Dancing hadn't been part of his plan for their short evening together, but holding her this way was even more pleasurable than he'd imagined. Graceful and pliant, she easily followed his lead, making him look like a much better dancer than he thought he was.

At first they moved with space between them, but it wasn't that kind of song. The sultry words of the vocalist made it seem natural for Ivy to cling to him, not resisting when his hand crept up her back and cradled her head on his shoulder.

She knew it was foolish to have romantic feelings about Rick, but being so close to him was incredibly sweet. Encouraged by the tenderness of his fingers caressing the back of her neck, she took her hand from the impersonally thick cloth on his shoulders and slid it under the back of his jacket, feeling the smoothness of his shirt and the warmth of his skin under it. With her eyes closed, all her other senses were doubling their efforts to know this man. His body heat was like a shield enveloping her, combining the spicy aroma of his aftershave with her own favorite cologne, Woodhue, so the very air around them seemed perfumed.

"You're light on your feet," he said softly.

"So long as I'm not light on yours." She knew it was the wrong time for a joke and was grateful when he held her a little tighter instead of rebuking her.

Why do they make songs so short? She'd love to dance until sunrise in Rick's arms.

"Let's go," he said when the number ended, leading her into the house to say good-bye to their host and hostess.

"So nice to have met you," Ivy said, wondering if Gretel would look so chic and intimidating without fifty pounds of jewelry. She tried to think of her as just another artist and complimented her earrings, feeling rewarded by a warm smile of thanks.

"I like Gretel," she said, sitting beside Rick in the station wagon as he drove along the secluded road, not making the turn back to the highway.

"So do I, but that's the kind of party where you should never have anything to do with the men."

"Is that why you took me there, to scare me with a wild and wicked bash?"

"That's putting it a little dramatically," he said. "I just want you to know there're a lot of people who'll try to take advantage of a woman."

"Men, you mean."

"Creeps who look good on the surface but have no scruples about misleading you."

"I'm sure there must've been some nice men at that party. Aren't we going home?" She had a good sense of direction, and noticed they weren't headed back toward Aragon.

"Not until I convince you not to be naive about the wrong kind of man."

"How can I tell who's right and who's wrong without encouraging them a little?"

He was gripping the steering wheel so hard, his fingers ached, at a loss to make her understand his warning.

"You start by avoiding the wrong parties—"

"There's that word again. I still don't know what was wrong with that one."

"The Ramons' parties get a little out of hand sometimes."

"People get drunk in Minnesota, too, you know."

"I wasn't kidding about the skinny-dipping."

"Really?" She'd never take her clothes off in front of strangers, not even to swim on a dark night, but the thought of Rick naked and running into the surf gave her a little rippling thrill. "Have you ever done it?"

"That's beside the point."

"I feel as if you're pushing my nose against the glass of a candy counter and telling me not to get fat," she said, pouting.

"Oh, Ivy." He laughed and pulled the car to a stop on the shoulder of the road, turning to take her face between his hands.

"Are there any other places where I should avoid men?" she whispered, feeling his fingers caress the sensitive skin below her ears.

"Singles bars." His voice was husky.

"And?"

"Parked cars." He leaned closer, covering her mouth with his and very, very slowly kissing first one corner of her lips and then the other.

"I can see that parked cars are dangerous," she said softly.

His thighs were trembling, and the blood seemed to have drained from his head, leaving him slightly giddy. "Let's take a walk," he murmured, pulling his hands away as if he'd been burned.

He stood alone outside the car for a long moment, pressing both palms against the fender, feeling as if his nervous system had just short-circuited. How could that little peck of a kiss leave him this shaky?

Ivy came up beside him, timidly reaching for his arm, following in silence as he led the way along the road. He knew the area well. Beyond the Ramon property there was a sharp outcrop of rock, then a patch of deserted beach, accessible only from above, a steep climb down to the shoreline. In need of a physical challenge to bring himself under control, he guided her in that direction.

The descent was steep, and he was cautious, going slowly so she wouldn't slip, although he soon realized that she was as surefooted as a young mountain goat. Alone together in the miniature cove, out of the range of civilized sounds and lights, he felt like the last man on earth, an eerie sensation that only made him more protective of the woman beside him.

"This is beautiful," she gasped, her voice so soft, he had to strain to hear it.

"The breeze is a little cool." He took off his jacket and laid it across her shoulders, keeping his arm there to hold it in place.

"Only because you're used to California heat," she said. "I'm warm; very warm."

She felt feverish, blood running hotly through her veins.

79

"I've never been in the ocean. Is the water cold?" she asked.

"Warmer than the Great Lakes, I imagine."

"I went into Lake Superior once. I thought I'd freeze to death." She kicked off her sandals, not even noticing where they went on the dark strip of sand.

Waves broke on the beach, then crept back to the sea, scouring the sand only inches from her nylon-clad feet.

"You're going to get wet," he warned, taking off his own shoes and socks.

"Turn your back," she said. "I'm going to take off my hose so I can wade."

She wadded the panty hose and stuffed them into her purse, feeling daring and free, walking forward to meet the slap of water on the shoreline.

"How is it?" he asked, remembering his fantasy, seeing her in his mind as a water nymph emerging from the crashing waves.

"Lovely." She dug her toes into the sand as foam-edged water swirled against her ankles. Catching at his hand, she said, "Come on."

"Wait." His fingers seemed too thick to unhook his slacks and work the zipper down, but he told himself it would be silly to get them wet. He stepped back to toss them on top of his jacket, adding his shirt to the pile but not his low-cut cotton briefs, white against tanned skin except for a pale strip around his middle usually covered by shorts.

Realizing what she'd started, Ivy froze beside the surf, wondering if she were capable of unsnapping the long row of snaps down the side of her dress. The decision was made for her.

"If you really want to go in you won't want to soak your dress."

He tentatively opened the uppermost snap, then the next and the next, feeling the warm texture of her arm, then the slinky softness of the camisole he'd insisted she buy.

He laid her dress on top of his clothes, stunned by the treasure of her body dimly revealed in the moonlight. Without conscious intention he stood in front of her, running his fingers down the thin straps of the silky camisole, tracing the dip of the neckline and sliding over the small mounds tipped by full, womanly nipples. His hands closed over them, electrified by the satiny friction of the garment, caressing and basking in her trembling acceptance of him.

"Never wear anything but this," he murmured, sliding his hands lower, feeling her taut little tummy and the fleshy swell of her buttocks in ruffled panties.

He felt like a virgin again, so awed by the mysteries of a female body that he touched her with reverence, holding his breath in suspenseful agony until he felt small hands exploring his torso, lithe fingers torturing his skin, sharp nails gliding through the mat of hair on his chest. Terrified of breaking the spell with words, he drew her into the protective circle of his arms, kissing her with a longing that surprised him.

His touch was the loveliest she'd ever felt, and his lips sizzled against her skin, exploring her closed lids, her throat, the top of her shoulder and the length of her arm. She didn't know her body had so many erotic spots, and when his tongue flicked against the sensitive skin of her inner wrist, she reached out in ecstasy, drawing his lips between hers with maddeningly pleasurable consequences.

She was poised on the threshold of discovery, all of her senses alive and demanding. With the fulfillment of her dreams so close, she was terrified, shaking in his arms, soothed by the same caresses that crazed her.

He felt the softness of her breasts, exposed when he threw aside the garment that had aroused him beyond the bounds of common sense. Her diminutive perfection made him feel large and clumsy, hovering over her, desperate to possess her. Dropping to his knees, he took her with him, feeling the gritty dryness of the sand, then standing again and scooping her into his arms.

He carried her only a few feet, and exertion had nothing to do with the harsh rasping of his breath. Taking her with him to the ground, he felt the caress of water on the hard-packed sand.

"It's not cold," she whispered, feeling the lick of the ocean on her back and thighs.

His mouth was devouring, taking possession of her breasts, exploring and arousing while she clutched at him with frenzied fingers, wanting him, needing him, loving him. . . .

Impatient with the few pieces of clothing that separated them, she wiggled out of her panties and helped him cast aside his briefs, loving the firm, cool flesh of his thighs and buttocks as he hovered over her, blinded, tormented, and baffled by a desire sharper and more agonizing than any he'd experienced.

In the back of his mind he'd expected inexperience, even reluctance, but Ivy's naturalness delighted him. She welcomed him without hesitation, so trusting that his heart swelled with tenderness, wanting more than anything to give her pleasure.

The undulation of her hips, washed by incoming waves, the softness of her thighs, the perfection of her calves were all unbearably seductive. His knees sank into the sand as he lowered himself over her, intoxicated by the erotic mingling of her sweet perfume with the scent of the sea. He filled her with himself, nurturing her soul and piercing her heart.

Beyond conscious thought, she still knew that this was the climax of her existence, the one moment that made everything that came before it a pale excuse for living.

Expecting everything, he was given even more, a pulsating, swelling, electrifying explosion that came as she cried out and dug her fingers into his back.

Had one sky ever held so many stars or one heart so much

feeling? She was dizzy with love, rocking on the shoreline of eternity, floating on a wavy sea of sensations. Rick lay beside her, letting the foamy surf beat against his shoulders and back, sheltering her in his arms and raining soft kisses on her face and neck.

"If we lie here forever, will we drown?" she murmured, making tiny circles on his chest with the tip of her finger, curling the wet whorls of hair down the length of his torso.

"I am drowning." He pressed his face against her wet hair and nibbled at her ear. "Drowning in you."

"Will you loan me your baby picture?" she asked shyly.

"My what?" He bent over her, wishing it were a sunny California morning, so he could see a golden glow on her skin and on the dark nipples still hard under his questing thumb.

"Baby picture. Do you have one on a bearskin rug?"

"I doubt that." He sat up, feeling the smile on her lips with his index finger. "What would you do with my baby picture?"

"I'm thinking of designing a boy doll."

He laughed uproariously, a deep rumble that started low in his chest and made him double over with mirth.

Then he stood abruptly, scooping her into his arms, feeling the sand clinging to her back, wading out through the surf, feeling his way carefully, skirting rough stones until he was standing chest-deep, braced against the pressure of the waves.

The enormity of the sea, so awesome to the landlocked, seemed to swell and rumble around her, but she'd never felt less fearful. She threw her arms around his neck and took him down with her into the ocean, sputtering, splashing, and kicking, washed back into his arms because that's where she wanted to be.

They frolicked and ducked each other, washing away the last traces of sand, until he picked her up again and carried her safely through the turbulence of breaking waves. Water streamed from their hair and gave their bodies a slippery glow in the moonlight. Too wet to dress, Ivy pressed against him in the circle of his arms, warmed and aroused again by his cool flesh against hers. She was in love with Rick. She buried her face against his shoulder, afraid of the depth of her caring.

Running his hands over her small shoulders, down the graceful line of her spine, over the soft swell of her buttocks, he wanted her again, hungry for her with an intensity he'd forgotten was possible. What was happening to him? He liked experienced, no-nonsense women, affairs with no strings attached, sex with no complications. Ivy was clinging to him, rubbing against him like a homeless kitten trying to woo a new master, exciting him beyond reason with her gentle caresses. He thought of spreading their clothes out on the sand and taking her again, but a wave of regret made him move her aside. She was looking for orange blossoms and honeymoons, promises and commitments, a husband and babies. None of these were for him, not now when he'd just decided to gamble on his first love: painting. He'd been a fool to get carried away by her shapely legs and beautiful breasts.

"We'd better get dressed," he said hoarsely, stepping away from her toward their pile of clothes.

Vigorous shaking failed to get rid of all the sand. Ivy had to put on her hose without panties because they were sodden and sandy, and Rick searched on hands and knees to find one of her sandals. They laughed a little self-consciously, joking about taking home enough grit to line Casey's cage.

The climb up the cliff was difficult, and in several places it took all of Rick's strength to pull Ivy up the sharp incline. The burden of her weight was easy to bear, but her trusting companionship tormented his conscience. Back in Minnesota her father would probably show up with a shotgun.

Here her gaiety and warmth told him that she was assuming much more than he was willing to give.

She cuddled against him on the ride home, dozing with her hand against the crease between his torso and thigh. Her touch was innocently arousing, but he accepted the discomfort as the beginning of his penance. He couldn't make love to her again and still face himself in the mirror. Somehow he had to let her know that their making love was a terrible mistake, one that was all his fault. He was selfish and depraved, inconsiderate and lecherous. For her own protection he had to make sure nothing like this happened again, but how could he do it without shattering her already fragile self-esteem? He ran a dozen possible excuses through his mind: a wife out of the country; insanity in the family; an incurable disease. None would do; with Ivy it had to be the truth or silence.

She stirred against him when he stopped in front of her house, awaking slowly because her dream was too precious to abandon. Remembering all that had happened, she knew reality could be better than fantasy.

Rick walked her to the door, but she didn't want to go in without him. Wrapping her arms around his back, she tilted her chin, expecting a kiss that didn't come.

"Would you like to come in?" she asked sleepily.

"You'd better get some sleep. I'll talk to you later."

Refusing her invitation was the hardest thing he'd ever done. Would it be so terrible to have a bed companion right in his own backyard? He knew it would be—for her.

"Rick." She paused, not knowing how to express what she wanted to say. "Thank you."

"Don't thank me, Ivy!" His protest was anguished, and he kissed her harshly.

Sure that anything he said then would lead to deeper trouble, he left her with a muffled "Good night."

CHAPTER FIVE

Rick worked furiously all day, determined to finish all the work he'd undertaken, getting the agency prints and the wedding portrait proofs ready to mail along with notes saying he'd be gone for a week or so. A neighbor across the road agreed to water his roses and take in the mail and newspapers. There was nothing to stop him from leaving early in the morning; he could mail the packaged photos at any post office along the route to his sister's home in Portland.

Trying to tell himself he was overdue for a visit with his niece and nephew didn't work. He was running away from a sticky situation and he knew it. The only question was: Should he say anything to Ivy before he left? Early in the evening he convinced himself it would be cowardly and cruel to disappear without a word. He picked six of his Lady X lavenders and surrounded them with John F. Kennedy roses, the strong fragrance of the pure white blooms making up for the light scent of the lavenders. The bouquet matched his subdued mood. He wished he could relive the evening he'd spent with Ivy at the beach but wasn't at all sure he could resist the sensual madness that had begun to sweep over him whenever he was near her. Filled with regrets, he thought all he could do now was try to let her down gently.

After a long, deep sleep, Ivy awoke, not quite believing the evening on the beach had been real in spite of the physical evidence: traces of sand in the bathtub left from her shower, damp panties, a rumpled dress, and sandals still gritty on the inside soles. Rick had made love to her along the water's edge, a wild, wonderful experience that left her still glowing with happiness.

Taking her morning coffee into the workroom, she cuddled up in a chair with a view of his house, reliving in her mind every astonishing minute of the night before. Everything about him pleased her. His face could be stern when he wanted to show authority, but when he looked at her with loving eyes, his features were beautiful, clean-lined, strong, and appealing. Hugging her arms across the front of her thin cotton nightie, she felt her nipples go hard at the thought of being with him. What an incredible sensation to have the ocean lapping against her naked body while the man she adored made love to her. Remembering made her want to run barefoot through his garden, picking enough roses to make a bed of soft, fragrant petals for the two of them.

Growing impatient with her imagination, she dressed for the day, putting on her new white shorts and a yellow silk blouse, wearing nothing under it. Rick was the only one who would see her today; he had to come over, knowing how much their lovemaking had meant to her. With her mind totally occupied by him, she took special care with her makeup and hair, happily anticipating the moment when he appeared at her back door.

A thousand times that day she looked out the windows of her workroom at the old fence and, beyond it, Rick's lovely rose garden, sure that he'd be there any minute. As her anxiety to see him grew, she remembered his flash of impatience when she'd tried to thank him for the evening. Had she done something to anger him? Was she only imagining that he'd enjoyed their lovemaking on the beach as much as she had?

As the day wore on doubts overwhelmed her. What had made her think Rick was pleased with her? She knew practically nothing about making love. A little pleasureless fumbling back in Minnesota certainly hadn't prepared her for a lover like Rick, and all the sweet things he'd murmured to her might have been sheer kindness, charity.

She worked in her yard, enduring the hot California sun, even though it was foolish to think Rick would see her trimming bushes and rush out to see her. Maybe he never wanted to see her again. Maybe it was true that men never respected an easy woman in the morning.

Nothing could be lonelier, Ivy thought, than wanting and waiting for a person who doesn't come.

The doll kit was finished. Ivy was in limbo, suffering as all creative people do when they're between projects without energy or ideas to begin something new. Just thinking about her request to borrow Rick's baby picture made her miserable with embarrassment. How could she have suggested modeling a boy doll after him? Had there been a full moon last night? She wanted to blame her romantic madness on something besides falling in love with Rick. Hadn't she known from the beginning that his lessons could be dangerous? He was a confirmed bachelor, devastatingly attractive to women and the last man for Ivy Gronsted of Ramsay, Minnesota. His absence probably meant that he was trying to think of some way to let her down easily.

She saw him coming, easily slipping over the fence with a bouquet of roses in hand. Wearing old, faded jeans and a knit shirt that looked forest green in the fading light, he moved slowly, stopping to rearrange some of the flowers. Ivy fell back into the shadows, unwilling to have him see her before he knocked.

She answered the door with a tentative little half-smile, accepting the roses with a quiet "thank you." Unfortunately she'd taken her lessons seriously; he noted unhappily that she'd never looked more beautiful or desirable. The yellow silk blouse she was wearing outlined her taut breasts and flattered her creamy skin. Trying not to imagine his lips roaming over her flawless skin, he remembered the speeches he'd practiced all afternoon, little fatherly talks that began with: "Ivy, you're a lovely young woman. I'll always cherish the gift you gave me last night."

The thought of saying something like that was suddenly disgusting to him, almost as bad as "Thank you, ma'am." In fact, he couldn't think of a single word to break the silence between them.

"Would you like to come in?" she offered, knowing that a refusal would trigger some uncontrollable weeping on her part.

"Thank you."

"I'd better put these in water. They're lovely, Rick."

"So are you."

You fool, he reprimanded himself silently. You're not supposed to say anything like that!

"Thank you," she said again, this time with a smile.

"You're welcome." He felt stiff and awkward.

These flowers she put in the workroom, a less elegant setting but more pleasing to him for some obscure reason. Did he want her to think of him while she worked on her dolls? That was terrible, too, completely contrary to his reason for coming to her house again.

"Ivy, I've been planning a trip to see my sister and her family. The kids are out of school now, and this is the best time for me to visit them. They'll be taking a vacation trip themselves in a few weeks. Maybe into Canada. They like to camp." Why was he telling her so much? he wondered.

Was he asking her to go along? Her momentary hope that he was quickly faded.

"So you see," he went on, "I'll be gone for a while, maybe a week, maybe two."

"Would you like me to bird-sit with Casey?" she asked dejectedly, doing a poor job of hiding her disappointment.

"Oh, no, thank you. He can come along this time. The kids love him."

89

"Yes, I imagine they do." Wasn't he going to say a word about last night? "Can I water your roses for you?"

"The neighbor across the street is doing that. We take turns watching each other's houses. It works out well for both of us." He silently cursed his own awkwardness, knowing he had to say something about the beach. "About last night . . ."

His evasiveness had already told her more than she wanted to know. The man standing in her workroom, who refused to sit down, wasn't there to tell her how much she meant to him. The only thing he could do that was worse was to apologize.

"Ivy, I'm sorry about last night."

The words nearly strangled him; the only thing he really regretted was not being able to make love to her again this minute, here on the bright plaid couch.

"I'm sorry it wasn't better. I guess I need to learn more than how to dress and apply makeup." She couldn't look at him.

Feeling trapped, he stepped closer and put his hands on both of her shoulders. If he told her how wonderful last night had been for him, would she assume they were beginning a relationship or, worse, expect a marriage proposal? Tilting her chin, he looked into her luminous blue-gray eyes, filling with tears, and knew he couldn't lie.

"It couldn't have been better," he said softly, thinking he'd rather be horsewhipped than destroy the trusting innocence of the woman in front of him. "You're a dynamite lady. I'm only sorry—"

"That you aren't in the market for anything permanent."

She had to end this devastating meeting; reading the truth on his face made it almost impossible to contain the tears building behind her eyes.

"Well, you'll want to get an early start in the morning," she said, anxious for him to leave before she broke down.

"Yes. But Ivy . . ."

He felt miserable, knowing that anything he said would make it worse for her. Against his better judgment he started to take her in his arms, but she stepped away from him.

"Well, thanks for the roses," she said, opening the door for him.

"You're very welcome."

Ivy pulled the drapes as soon as he left, not wanting him to look back and see her. There's no such thing as a good cry, she decided, burying her face in a wad of tissues and sobbing until her head throbbed and her eyes burned.

On Monday morning Ivy resolved to design a doll that was uniquely different, a project so completely absorbing that she wouldn't have time to think about Rick. She pulled out every reference book she owned on old dolls, studying them page by page, searching for the inspiration she needed. Skimming through the section on baby dolls, she knew it would be nearly impossible to improve on some of the old favorites: EFFanBEE, Bye-Lo, Kestner, Armand Marseille. The mechanicals—talkers, walkers, drinkers, and wetters— were largely designed by people with mechanical talent, which she didn't have. The fashion dolls by French and German makers were exquisite but didn't offer the kind of challenge she needed.

Coming to a picture of her all-time favorite doll, Heubach's character doll of an old American Indian woman with eyes so real, they seemed to be moist, she stared at it for a long time. She didn't own this doll but had seen several examples in doll museums. Would a beautifully designed and costumed ethnic doll sell well today? Visualizing a doll dressed in a Norwegian folk costume kindled her enthusiasm. Collectors were a natural market for this type of doll, but wasn't it time for a mass market line to dramatize the cultural heritage of the United States? Her agent and the toy manufacturers might disagree, but she had nothing to lose by designing a model for a whole line of ethnic dolls. Her first would be a little Norwegian girl, a bit slimmer and older than Karol Ann but still a child. She'd need to find a lovely seven- or eight-year-old to serve as the model; maybe her friend at the library knew some teachers who could help her get the photos she needed. Researching and designing the first costume would be time-consuming, so she decided it would definitely be Norwegian, since she'd had experience in making her own full-size outfit.

Usually when she began a new project, she was seized by feverish excitement, so eager to begin that everything else seemed unimportant. It was the same creative frenzy that touched painters, writers, inventors, composers, anyone who built upon the imaginings of the mind. She started her research with her own library, hoping to be engulfed by the project, depending on her new idea to push all thoughts of Rick out of her mind.

Unfortunately this didn't happen. After three days of intensive work, finding a neighborhood little girl to pose for photographs, taking notes, assembling materials, and doing some tentative modeling in clay, she still thought of Rick constantly. Her project was off to a good start, thanks largely to her disciplined work habits, but she had Rick on her mind all the time, still hurting because she knew he'd gone away to avoid her.

Wednesday evening she went to a meeting of the art group, rather relieved that Nate wasn't there, and Saturday all the members of the Norwegian Society were invited to a wedding of two of the members. She wore her folk costume, as did several other women, and at least there it was appreciated. Her life was full and interesting, but nothing seemed to fill the emptiness in her heart.

Jenny and Todd kept Rick busy playing games, his sister Beth fussed over him like a mother hen, and Steve, his brother-in-law, took him along for an evening of poker with friends. Rick enjoyed his sister's family, but he was restless, wishing he could cut short the visit without hurting their feelings. At first he told himself it was the chance to paint full-time that made him so eager to return to Aragon. By Sunday he admitted that he was worried about his neighbor. He never should have interfered in Ivy's life, but since he had, he felt responsible for her and more than a little guilty for letting things go so far that evening on the beach.

The answer came to him as he was approaching Santa Barbara, for no particular reason except that Ivy was on his mind as he drove. Single and living alone, she was always going to seem defenseless and vulnerable to him. Since he had no intention of moving from his home, the answer was simple: Ivy had to get married. Once she settled down with some nice guy, which was what she wanted, he would forget her. He'd originally offered to give her some guidance because she seemed so ill-equipped to deal with men; if he helped her meet someone suitable, his feeling of responsibility would end.

The idea of matchmaking made him uncomfortable, but accidental meetings between Ivy and a few of his friends wouldn't be difficult to arrange. All he had to do was make a list of prospects, see that Ivy met them, and let nature take its course. It probably wouldn't be that simple, but taking action would be better than stewing in his guilt. Ivy was lovely in a fragile, haunting way, unspoiled and unpretentious. He forced himself to remember her at their first meeting, awkwardly stepping around the spilled scrub water, her hair tied back in a lank ponytail. If he dwelled on what had happened at the beach, the impression of her hips in the damp sand in the instant before the surf washed over it and the granules sticking to her smooth limbs as he carried her into the sea, then his plan would fail.

By the time he reached home he had a list of three prospects for her, two solid and one maybe. Artists, photographers, and men in show business—the majority of his friends —were out. Ivy needed someone mature, stable, and dependable. His tax accountant had just taken in a new partner, something Davis, yes, Tom Davis: thirty or so, single, presentable, smart. Tony VanderVos was his second choice. A widower since his wife's fatal car crash four years ago, Tony probably was ready for a new serious relationship. His third possibility was Ned Linson, an account executive at the agency that contracted for Rick's work. Linson might be a year or two younger than Ivy, but Rick was sure he would welcome a date with a woman shorter than himself. Tonight Rick was too tired, but first thing in the morning he'd go through his address book and the business cards he kept filed in his desk for other likely candidates.

His bed felt good after the hide-a-bed at Beth's house. He should've fallen asleep immediately, beat as he was after a weekend of camping and the long trip home. Instead, at one a.m. he was looking down on Ivy's house, dark now, thinking things that had nothing to do with his plans for her future.

Rick was back. She saw him unwinding a hose to soak the roses before the sun was high. Shirtless, dressed only in old jeans and running shoes, he pulled the green coils, tamed them to snake around the thirsty bushes, the muscles on his well-tanned back rippling. What she really wanted to see were his eyes, to read there what he really thought of her. Was he as indifferent as his week-long absence suggested? Was making love only a casual Saturday night activity for him? She wanted a reason to hope but didn't expect to find one.

He had planned to paint but cut a sampler bouquet of all his roses instead and took it to Ivy after he'd showered, shaved, and eaten breakfast.

Longing to see him, she found herself tongue-tied when he actually came to her back door carrying a magnificent bouquet of roses: apricot, yellow, red, white, pink, and the precious lavender.

"One of each." His mouth smiled, but his eyes were wary.

She accepted the flowers, knowing she should say something, but she was unable to wrench any sound from her constricted throat. Carrying them silently to the kitchen to find a vase, she knew he was following, expecting something from her.

"I got back late yesterday." He frowned, not liking the obligation he felt to account for his time. "A week with my sister's family is fun, but those kids really wear me out. I think even Casey is pooped."

"These are beautiful." She plunked the whole bouquet into her largest vase, a plain clear glass, without attempting to rearrange them artfully. "Thank you."

"You're welcome."

She looked angry; he knew better than to get involved with a woman who expected sex to be the beginning of a thrilling new relationship. He found her coolness maddening. If she wanted to berate him, let her do it with words. He could handle accusations and tantrums; he'd proved that in Vegas with Biffy. But Ivy's silence was driving him crazy.

"Come here." He took her hand, so small and soft in his, and led her into the living room, insisting that she sit beside him on the couch.

"I am in the middle of a project, Rick. An idea for a series of ethnic dolls."

"I won't take much of your time. We have to talk, you know."

She didn't help him by asking questions.

"On the beach . . ." he began awkwardly.

"That's past. It didn't mean anything, so I'd rather just forget it."

She'd never forget it, she knew, but hearing him apologize again was more than she could bear. Why couldn't he leave her alone if he didn't love her?

He was never going to forget it. Just thinking about it, he could taste the sweetness of her lips and the salty tang of skin washed by the ocean.

"I'd hate to think we're not still friends," he said softly.

"Of course, we're friends," she lied, miserable because

95

she knew they had to have much more than friendship, or nothing.

"You were wonderful, Ivy. Warm, giving . . ." He almost said "loving" but stopped himself.

"Rick, I don't want to talk about it."

Her harsh words were like a slap in the face. A much deserved slap, he thought.

"Will you do one thing for me?" He was gambling on her generous nature.

"If I can," she said wearily, aching to be in his arms and wanting him to leave because she knew she'd never experience that pleasure again.

"Come to a small party at my place on Saturday evening. I'll burn some steaks on the grill outside. Just a few old friends."

"Couples like the Ramons?"

"No, a quieter crowd, mostly single."

"I don't think so, Rick."

"Do you have other plans?"

"No, but—"

"Ivy, we live awfully close. If you're really not upset about what happened at the beach . . ."

"I'm not!" she insisted defensively.

"Then come. Please."

"No more lessons?" What she'd learned on their practice date had disrupted her life.

"None, I promise. Just a few nice friends, some of the people from the accounting firm that does my taxes. You may need someone locally to do yours." He hoped Davis was available Saturday night.

"I guess I will."

"That means you'll come?"

She didn't want to, but refusing seemed boorish. If they cooked and ate outside, she'd have to see and hear them, anyway.

"Yes, for a little while. I won't stay late."

"Wonderful. Wear your champagne silk."

"For a cookout?" She thought life in California was supposed to be casual. "I thought my lessons were over!"

"Wear it if you want to," he said lamely.

Rick was right about wearing the dress. The first guests, a man and a woman, arrived in a white linen suit and an emerald crepe evening dress, wandered through the garden, then settled down under a yellow striped umbrella on his patio. She could see them from her back window, but in order to get there without snagging her dress or hose, she chose to drive the back way, two miles of narrow, twisting roads. Rick was welcome to his rickety old fence, because this was the last time she expected to go to his house by car or by foot. Accepting his invitation was a mistake she'd regretted every waking minute since he'd invited her. A dozen times she'd stood by the phone intending to call and cancel, but her pride wouldn't let her. She wasn't afraid of Rick Winterset, and she wasn't going to be a coward and hide at home behind closed drapes while he entertained.

By the time she locked the house, leaving a night-light on, and drove to his place, she was the last to arrive. It was a small party: Willard and Mary Hodgkins, the head accountant in the firm Rick used and his wife; Tom Davis, the junior partner; and Fran Simmons, a bony, dark-complexioned woman in her forties who lived down the road and ran a gift and card shop in Aragon. Fran seemed the ideal woman to fill in at parties: gracious, friendly, and talkative but obviously older than either Rick or Tom. Ivy wasn't terribly surprised when Fran acted as unofficial hostess, leaving her free to talk to the other guests. And she didn't need to be a wizard to guess what Rick was up to when Tom started to monopolize her, talking a blue streak about tax shelters and write-offs, undaunted by the fact that Ivy lost the gist of what he was saying most of the time.

"You look terrific," Rick said softly, wearing an apron and

a tall chef's hat, distributing steaks from the grill to guests holding heavy stoneware platters.

"Thank you, but I know what you're doing," she hissed under her breath.

A slight breeze and several bug control devices kept the yard comfortable and free of mosquitoes, and the small party lingered there over potent rum drinks for hours after dark. Ivy was the only one not interested in sheltered annuities and long-term capital gains, although the combined urgings of the three men did convince her that she needed professional help to manage the comfortable income from her royalties. There was no guarantee that future years would bring such substantial profits once the enthusiasm for Karol Ann waned.

She wasn't used to drinking, but Tom kept refilling her glass; the rum drink was deceptively sweet, going down easily but packing an unexpected wallop. Losing all compulsion to participate, she let the conversation go over her head, aware only of Rick, stretched out on a lounge chair opposite her, one leg drawn up in pale fawn slacks that fit like a glove. He grew more quiet, too, drinking less than his guests but keeping a pitcher full for them along with a bowl of salty snacks. After the heavy meal of steak, baked potatoes, and Caesar salad, Ivy had no interest in corn chips or peanuts. Maybe because she didn't nibble, the rum seemed to go to her head. When the others finally rose to leave, she felt as if the ground were rocking under her feet.

"Sit down and stay there," Rick ordered in a low voice, then walked the others to their cars.

She needed a minute to clear her head, but she walked unsteadily around the rose garden instead of staying in the cushioned lawn chair. Rick seemed to return almost immediately.

"You'd better go home over the fence. Those drinks have hit you pretty hard. You can pick up your car tomorrow."

He sounded mildly amused, which made her a little belligerent.

"I'll ruin my dress on that awful old fence. I can drive."

"Not tonight you can't," he said more sternly. "You can sleep here or go home over the fence."

She wasn't too inebriated to know that it wasn't an invitation to share his bed. The thought of waking up on his couch because she'd drunk too much to go home was almost enough to make her sober.

"I'll walk home," she said crossly.

"I'll see you to your door."

"Not necessary."

She walked between the rose beds with exaggerated care, determined not to let her neighbor see her fall. The lights from his patio didn't reach to the fence, and she heard a ripping sound as soon as she put her foot on the first crosspiece board. The nylon over her shin had snagged.

"Great idea," she muttered to Rick, who was just behind her. "I've already torn my hose."

"I'm sorry. You should've waited for me to give you a boost."

"I'm not going to ruin my dress. I'll drive the long way."

"No chance." He blocked her retreat with his body. "There's a much simpler solution."

"What?" Her voice sounded like someone else's.

"Just take off your dress and I'll hand it over to you."

"Oh, no."

"It's dark. I can't even see you. And I promise, Ivy, you're safe with me."

"But not with myself," she said so softly, he asked her to repeat it. She didn't.

Hating to sacrifice her lovely dress, she started over the fence again, but Rick's arms captured her from behind, setting her firmly down on both feet, still on his side of the barrier.

99

"Don't be silly. I know what you paid for that dress. It was worth it."

He reached out and found the zipper running the length of her back, carefully lowering the tab, not touching the expanse of bare skin under it. The full, silky folds in front had tempted her to go braless with only a half-slip, something she'd never have done before meeting Rick. He lifted the hem, bringing it over her head. She quickly crossed her arms over her breasts, the alcoholic fog dissipating as embarrassment flooded her senses.

"I knew you weren't wearing one," he teased. "Now climb over carefully. I already owe you new hose."

Just once he'd like to see all of her under bright lights, but tonight the darkness was his ally. No resolution in the world could govern his response to her, not in that instant when he drew the dress over her head and she stood exposed. He handed the garment to her as soon as she was in her own yard.

"Put it on," he ordered unnecessarily, following her over the fence, heedless of his own good slacks.

"I can see myself in," she insisted.

"Not if your keys are in this purse." He dangled it from one finger.

"Why are you going out of your way to make me feel foolish?" She sounded weepy.

Why was he? He was angry about her drinking, frustrated because she sat beside Tom all night letting him refill her glass over and over again from the icy pitcher which, as the host, he felt obligated to replenish. Because he rarely entertained them, he'd forgotten that the Hodgkinses were heavy drinkers. It wasn't surprising that the new partner could keep up with them, but that was no excuse for Davis to press liquor on Ivy. He should've noticed that she wasn't used to it.

Anyway, Rick thought with annoyance, he could scratch

100

Davis from the list. At least the party had been at his house; that jerk could be driving half-crocked with Ivy in his car.

"I'm not making you feel anything," he said, cross with her because he was mad at himself. "Let me get the door."

"I can."

"Are we going to argue about it?"

"You're treating me like a child!"

"No, like a mature woman who's too drunk to drive home," he said sarcastically.

"It was your party, your drinks, your friend who kept refilling my glass and saying what weak drinks they were!"

"Davis said that?" He was thinking of looking for a new tax firm to handle his business.

She stepped inside the door after he opened it and tried to rezip her dress in the dim light spilling into the workroom from the hallway. He turned on the overhead lights, not sorry he had when he saw the creamy skin of her back beside the shimmery champagne silk. Itching to run his fingers down her spine and feel the softness of her skin, he scratched his chin instead, reddening it with the vigor of his quest for relief.

"Ivy."

An undertone of urgency in his voice made her swing around to face him.

"Thank you for a lovely evening," she said woodenly.

"You didn't have a lovely time," he said, cupping her chin in his fingers.

"No, I didn't." She could admit this much without letting him know what torture it had been to have him so near and yet so far.

"I'm sorry." He was deeply regretting his failed attempt at matchmaking. Next time he'd choose more wisely, and he wouldn't be a third party, watching in misery while some bum tried to—

"No, don't be sorry," she said, interrupting his thought.

"I know what you're trying to do, and I appreciate it. Better luck next time."

"I thought you'd like Tom."

"Well, I didn't. Not much, anyway. Just drop it, will you, Rick? I don't think I'm going to graduate from your charm school."

"You already have a master's degree," he said, bending to brush her forehead with his lips, then leaving as quickly as he could.

CHAPTER SIX

She awoke with a headache that throbbed all the way to her
jaw, and Mary Alice Hallingdal was picking her up for an
outdoor church service in an hour. She thought of calling to
cancel, but they'd made the plans last week at the wedding.
Mary Alice was a nurse and often worked weekends; it
wouldn't be fair to spoil her day.

Somehow Ivy managed to be ready, dressed in her pink
shirtwaist dress with her hair fluffed and eye shadow laid
thick to partially disguise her bleak eyes, when Mary Alice
arrived in her sand-colored Citation. With neat ash-blond
curls surrounding a cheerful, round face, Mary Alice was one
of the few people in California who reminded Ivy of her
friends in Minnesota. Slightly on the plump side, she dis-
guised her girth with some success by wearing dark colors;
this morning her navy linen sheath had the crispness of a
military uniform.

"Ready for our big day?" Mary Alice asked when Ivy slid
into the car.

"Hopefully."

"I thought we could have lunch at this great little organic
food shop. Their brown rice and mushroom balls are really
good, and I love tomatoes stuffed with spicy avocado paste.
Or you might want to try goat cheese on rye with marinated
mushrooms, or—"

"Won't we miss all the good buys if we waste time eating

before we go to the flea market?" Ivy asked, realizing that her stomach felt a little queasy.

"We could go there right after the service." Mary Alice was always agreeable. "If you don't want organic food I know a guy who waits tables at a Russian restaurant. All the waiters have big, bushy black beards, and their cabbage rolls with sour cream and black olives are delicious. Or we could have kidney soup. I'm not crazy about it, but you should try it once."

"Mary Alice, please! I haven't even had breakfast!"

"Are you feeling all right, Ivy?" She squinted at her with a professional eye.

"Not great. I went to a cookout at my neighbor's house last night. I didn't realize there was so much rum in a drink that tasted like citrus punch."

"That's too bad. Drink a lot of water and juice and you'll feel better. Was it a big party?"

"No, only my neighbor and a few of his friends. Will we be late?"

"No, I allowed plenty of time. Is your neighbor single?"

"Yes."

"Available?"

Now she knew why Mary Alice reminded her of friends at home.

"Not for me," Ivy answered.

"How can you be sure?"

"If he's interested in me he sure has a funny way of showing it."

"What do you mean?"

"He's trying to help me find a husband!"

Mary Alice laughed loudly, swerving into the adjacent lane.

"Watch your driving!" Mary Alice hadn't endangered them, and Ivy hadn't snapped because of her driving. "I'm sorry. Just forget I said that."

"I'm not likely to forget that you have a male neighbor

104

who's trying to find a husband for you. I should live in a neighborhood like that!"

"I exaggerated. He only introduced me to an accountant, and I didn't like him very much."

"Oh." Her friend sounded disappointed. "My cousin is coming out to stay with my folks this summer. Would you like to meet him?"

"I'm not very enthusiastic about blind dates."

"It doesn't have to be a blind date. I'll bring him to the Norwegian Society meeting. If you like each other it's up to you to get better acquainted."

Without any real interest Ivy asked, "Why is he coming?"

"My dad thinks he can get him a job here. Things aren't exactly booming in Wisconsin. Thank heavens Dad went into computers when he did. I'd still be paying for my education if we'd stayed in Olsonville."

It turned out to be a nice day. Hearing familiar, inspirational words in a tranquil outdoor setting was deeply satisfying, and Mary Alice was a pleasant companion, good-natured and easygoing like Ivy's old friends in Ramsay. After the service they wandered for hours through acres of flea market, and Ivy bought a big box of felt scraps that were sure to come in handy as she designed her ethnic costumes.

Famished by then, they settled for a late-afternoon supper at a small family-owned café in Aragon. They had big slices of sweet potato pie with old-fashioned fried chicken and sliced tomatoes on lettuce, followed by rice pudding, a treat Ivy hadn't had since early childhood when her family visited her Aunt Irene.

When she got home, her headache was gone, and her friendship with Mary Alice was on firm ground. There was no reason to feel as dejected as she did.

After a long soak in hot, scented water, she felt worse. For the first time since moving she was homesick, nostalgic about her uncomplicated life at home. She phoned her parents, which didn't help much, since they showered her with concern, worried about her reckless new life-style. Then she tried Vi, who wasn't home, and when she called her other sister, she learned Iris had a houseful of company, her once-a-month bridge club, and couldn't talk. Ivy always forgot about the time difference.

Sorting through the felt she'd bought at the flea market, she made neat piles of different colored pieces that looked like remnants from a factory that made souvenir pennants. With a little embroidery the bright red would make nice suspenders for the Norwegian doll. Usually she named her dolls as she created them, but so far no name for this one had come to her. Maybe the membership list for the Norwegian Society would inspire her, but she didn't feel like reading it.

Going to bed early was no cure for what ailed her; with no other distractions she lay for long hours thinking about Rick. She might as well have stayed in Minnesota. Someone there always had a cousin for her to meet, too.

By placing his easel between two rose beds, Rick achieved exactly the view he wanted: rolling hills beginning to turn yellow under a hot sun with the trellis of Royal Sunset climbers, the bright apricot blooms Ivy had admired, fading to a creamy white in the heat. It wasn't the first time he'd painted a blooming bush, but he still smarted under her challenge. Why didn't he try to capture the delicate shades he loved in a floral still life?

On impulse he moved the easel to include a back corner of her house in the scene he planned to paint. The ruddy shade of the tiled roof was just the contrast he needed. He went to work, looking more often than necessary at the snug little bungalow that looked deserted this afternoon. It'd been ten long days since his fiasco of a party, and somehow he and Ivy hadn't seen each other, not even for a wave over the fence. Even if she was slaving on a new project, didn't she ever come out for a whiff of fresh air?

She saw him, of course. She always did, whether he was puttering in his garden or painting. There were probably a dozen excuses for going into her backyard, but she stayed inside, away from the one person she most wanted to see. Struggling with the hair of her new doll, working and re-working a pale-blond style, trying to avoid a straight, chopped look and still making it look authentic, she couldn't seem to get it right. Walking to the window, she stood at the side, hoping the shadowed interior of her workroom would conceal her from the man painting in the bright sunlight. What was he wearing on his head? It looked like a fisherman's cotton hat with trout lures pinned on it. Well, at least he had enough sense to shield his head in this heat.

He looked in her direction and waved; she felt silly spying on him from the edge of the window. Worse, he was walking in her direction, springing over the fence with ease.

"Hello," he called. He didn't have a reason for being at her door but hoped she'd be in a hospitable mood.

"Hi."

"Can I come in?"

"Sure."

"You're not too busy?"

"No, I'm at an impasse. I can't get my doll's hair just the way I want it."

"My landscape isn't going well, either. Wish I'd painted the Royal Sunsets earlier in the season."

"The big orange-colored roses?"

"Yes." He was inside but didn't know why he wanted to be there.

"Would you like some lemonade, fresh-squeezed? I also have some Norwegian beer."

"Lemonade sounds great."

He followed her into the kitchen, a small, cheerful room with a cherry-red stove and refrigerator, red and blue baskets silhouetted on white wallpaper, and marbleized blue floor covering. The small scrubbed-pine table looked inviting, so he sat on one of the spindle-backed chairs beside it.

She made every move with brisk efficiency, and he wondered why he'd ever thought she was klutzy just because of a spilled pail that had tipped over because he startled her.

"You look nice," he said, enjoying the bare length of her legs in bright yellow shorts.

"Thank you." She sounded surprised, caught off guard by his simple compliment. "You deserve the credit, of course."

He thought of telling her he'd had nothing to do with her shapely legs and beautiful bones, but he didn't want their conversation to proceed in that direction. "All I did was introduce you to Sincerely."

"No, you did more." She didn't want to go into details. The most important thing he'd done was to make her feel beautiful.

"I feel as if I've let you down." He hadn't encouraged her to look better so she could attract a man like Davis, that was for sure.

"No, not at all. I have vanilla wafers," she stated in an effort to change the subject. "Would you like some?"

"Cookies aren't one of my vices." He smiled broadly. "I do have one more suggestion, though."

"If it has anything to do with blind dates . . ."

"Not exactly. I just want to do a favor for a friend." This time he'd be subtle. "He's in charge of the Aragon Street Art Fair for next year. He's desperate for an unusual way to publicize it. I suggested a doll, a symbol for the show that could only be purchased there."

"A limited edition, you mean?"

"Exactly."

Tony VanderVos wasn't imaginative enough himself to turn down a good suggestion. Rick was confident that he could get his friend at the bank at least to consider commissioning Ivy to design a doll. If something developed from there who could accuse him of matchmaking?

"I suppose it's possible, if I have enough notice ahead of time."

"More than ten months?"

"No, not that much. A cloth doll, maybe. I could hire local help to assemble them."

"The economy here can always use a boost."

"I don't imagine your friend would need enough to make a difference in the unemployment rate."

He told her more about the art show, then accepted a second glass of lemonade, thinking how pleasant it would be to take her out for dinner and a drive along the ocean, maybe a movie or an excursion to L.A. for some night life. But that would only intensify his preoccupation with her: daytime fantasies that interfered with his painting. If he didn't feel as if he'd made some progress in his art by the end of the summer, he'd accept photographic assignments again in the fall, a return to commercial life that he didn't look forward to. His job now was to convince Tony that the art fair needed a doll as a promotion piece. He'd probably think it was a goofy idea—until he met Ivy.

Convincing the bank vice-president had been tougher than getting Ivy interested in his idea, but Rick finally arranged a meeting between them, cautioning his friend to make it sound like his own idea. He had to see Ivy's work to appreciate it, Rick insisted, so he took Tony to her house on a Thursday evening, planning to leave as soon as their conversation got rolling.

As soon as she saw Tony VanderVos, Ivy knew what Rick was doing: scheming to pair her off with another of his friends. The banker was lanky and dark-haired with rather craggy features, but he had a wide smile. She liked him well enough on first sight, but her displeasure with Rick grew stronger. She already knew he wasn't interested in her. Why did he parade his friends in front of her like entries in a dog show? Didn't he think she was capable of meeting men on her own?

109

"Now that I've seen what you can do, I'm sold on the idea, Ivy," Tony said some time later. "When can we get together to talk business, prices, numbers, deadlines, that sort of thing?"

"Whenever you like." She was being as charming as she could, noticing that Rick was so quiet, he seemed sulky. Why didn't he just go home? It was awkward to have him hovering over her like a mother hen.

"How about tomorrow evening?"

"That would be fine."

"I probably won't get away from the bank until around six. Would you mind if we have dinner first, say I pick you up at seven?"

"I'll look forward to it," she replied with a smile.

She also looked forward to telling Rick what she thought of his heavy-handed manipulating. He'd waved his magic wand, and now she was Cinderella on her way to the ball. He didn't have to stay around to see if the glass slipper fit.

Tony left, but her neighbor didn't.

"The doll idea was an excuse to have me meet your friend, wasn't it?" she asked suspiciously, walking over to the wrought-iron couch where Rick was lounging with posed nonchalance.

"Tony needed a good idea."

"You are not my agent, Rick. I have all the work I need."

"You can refuse him."

"But I probably won't, if he's serious about a limited edition. I always feel I should contribute something to the community where I live."

"Doll making is your business," Rick reminded her.

"Yes, but I sell my designs to manufacturers. I wouldn't dream of making a profit when the proceeds of the art show are going to a good cause."

"If I sell any paintings I intend to keep the money."

"What about your Aragon street scene that you're donating to the show?"

110

"One donation." He shrugged his shoulders and stood to leave.

"Don't try to fix me up with anyone else, Rick."

"Tony's a nice guy. Lonesome since his wife was killed in a car accident four years ago."

"I've seen him in the bank. We might've gotten acquainted on our own."

"Ivy, we're friends, aren't we?"

She didn't answer.

"Tony will probably show up in a three-piece suit, but he likes a little flamboyance in his women. Wear the dress with the stripes. And don't go to an Italian restaurant. He and his first wife went to Mario's all the time. You don't want to compete with a memory."

"Wear zebra stripes! Don't eat Italian food! Listen to you, Rick! Do you really think that's going to have anything to do with whether Tony and I become friends?"

"Probably not," he admitted. "All you really need is more confidence. I'm only trying to help you gain it."

"You're not succeeding!"

"I'm sorry. Just don't talk about the Norwegian Society and Minnesota, and let him find out for himself what a nice person you are."

"Oh, Rick!" She wanted to throw something at him. "I know what you want me to be: sophisticated. I don't think clothes and makeup and small talk are going to do it. I'm me, and this date isn't going to be any different from all the others I've gone on. Men never ask me out a second time!"

He didn't believe she'd intentionally make him feel like a heel, but he did. Her face revealed her self-doubt and hurt, making him want to take her into his arms, but he couldn't offer her false security. He wasn't always going to be there to soothe away her hurts, and that was what she needed: a man who would cherish her forever. His plan to provide one was backfiring, and he felt as miserable as she did.

"Only because you discourage them," he said softly, "and I don't know why you do."

"Go home, Rick," she said peremptorily.

"Ivy, I didn't bring Tony here to hurt you."

"I know. Just go."

"Ivy . . ." He wanted to make her understand.

"Go, Rick!"

This time she watched dry-eyed as he crossed the fence and garden. Maybe her dismal record with men wasn't all her fault. They could be incredibly dense sometimes, especially her interfering neighbor.

Rick was wrong about the three-piece suit, just as he'd misjudged his friend in more important ways. Tony came to her door wearing skin-tight blue jeans and a long-sleeved black shirt. A heavy gold chain nestled seductively in the heavy mat of hair that peeked through his halfway unbuttoned shirt. The last thing on his mind was Italian food.

"I thought we could pick up some Chinese food and take it back to my place," he said with a grin that wasn't boyish.

"I don't think so, Tony."

"I have all the budget material for the art fair there," he insisted. "I live in the Marble Gardens apartments, you know, the luxury condominiums right on the beach."

"We could just talk in a general way," she suggested. "The café in town's not bad at all. My friend and I had dinner there."

"I eat lunch there three times a week," he said, laughing softly. "You're not afraid to come to my place, are you?"

"Of course not. You are Rick's friend. He gave you high recommendations."

"Nice of him." Tony was still smiling as he opened the door of his Porsche for her.

Ivy decided to go along with Tony's plan, but if this friend of Rick's wasn't on the level, Rick would hear about it, she vowed.

Tony's living room was sparsely furnished with a modern

brown velvet love seat and matching chair, and a chrome-and-glass coffee table. A movie-screen-size television filled one corner of the room. It took her a minute to realize that there wasn't a personal possession in sight, not a single knickknack, book, or photograph. The one decoration on the walls was a brown-and-white abstract painting that she found rather ugly. It was hard to believe that anyone would live willingly in such a sterile, unimaginative room. She wondered if the shock of his wife's death had made Tony lose interest in his home.

"Kitchen's through here," he said, laying his hand on her shoulder.

This room, too, was impersonally furnished with the minimum number of utilitarian pieces.

"Do you rent furnished?" she asked.

"No," he answered, looking at her quizzically. "I'll get some plates. What would you like to drink?"

"Coffee is fine."

"Sorry, I'm out. I have beer, Scotch, or vodka."

"Maybe just a glass of water, then." The emptiness of his apartment, more than the air conditioning, was giving her a chill.

Twice while they sat on the love seat eating the contents of several cardboard cartons with wire handles, she tried to discuss the art fair and the doll idea.

"Let's talk later," he said with a grin that no longer seemed pleasant.

"I am so full," she exaggerated, pushing away her less than half-eaten plate of food, getting up with the intention of refilling her water glass.

He was too quick for her, jumping up and blocking her way to the kitchen.

"I'm really glad you're here tonight," he said quietly, stroking her cheek with the backs of his fingers.

"I can't stay long. We really should talk about the doll now."

113

"Later." He captured her between his arms and held the back of her head, kissing her hungrily.

"No." She pushed at his chest but couldn't break free.

"It gets so lonesome, being by myself," he said in a way that convinced her he often used that line.

"I live alone and like it," she insisted.

"Because you don't know what you're missing." He pulled her against him, covering her mouth with wet kisses.

"Stop it!" She struggled free, digging her fist into the soft spot below his rib cage.

"I think this art fair could be a good thing for you, sweetheart," he said, trying another tactic.

"Forget it! I'm leaving."

"Leave, then. Have a nice walk."

He made her push past him, fondling her breast as she did. "You're making a mistake. We could have a nice time."

Too angry to speak, she slammed the door as an answer and ran to the elevator.

It wasn't dark yet, and the last thing Ivy wanted to do was knock on a stranger's door asking to use a phone. Who could come for her, anyway? There was no such thing as taxi service in Aragon. She started walking, trying to figure how far she was from home. It could be as much as five miles, and her feet hurt already in the high heels she'd bought to wear with her zebra-striped dress.

There was a service station a few hundred yards ahead, and she knew it would be dark before she walked all the way home, even if her feet could take the punishment. Rick got her into this mess; let him get her out.

At the station pay phone she dialed his number, listening to it ring again and again. How did Rick spend his evenings? He could be out; he could have company. He might be very busy with one special guest. Tormented by all the things she didn't know about him, she let the phone keep ringing, no longer expecting an answer but unwilling to sever the connection.

"Hello." He sounded out of breath.

"Rick, it's Ivy. I rang and rang."

"So I heard," he said dryly. "I was outside."

"You've got to come and get me!"

"What's wrong?" he asked urgently.

"It wasn't a very successful evening. Please come now, Rick."

"Right away. Where are you?"

"You know where Marble Gardens is?"

"Where Tony lives?"

"Yes, I'm at a station about a mile away. It's a self-service place with a cowboy on the sign."

"I know the one. Go inside, Ivy. Stay by the cashier. I'm on my way."

The station attendant was enthroned behind glass with only an opening for cash and credit cards. It was too complicated to ask him for sanctuary, but she stood beside the building in his line of vision until Rick's station wagon pulled in, scattering dust behind the rear wheels.

"Are you okay?" He jumped out and put his arm around her.

She'd rehearsed all kinds of scathing things to say about his choice of escorts but instead found herself reassuring him.

"Of course, he didn't do anything to me. Except refuse to drive me home."

"Why?" He guided her into the car, standing by the open passenger door.

"Can we go?" she asked.

"Yes, but I want to know why you're out here alone."

He sat behind the wheel with the motor running, waiting for her to explain.

"You're wasting gas."

"What happened, Ivy?"

"He said we should have dinner at his apartment because all his art fair information was there."

115

"You believed him?"

"He's a friend of yours!"

"Then what?"

"He bought some Chinese food, and we went back there to eat it. Have you ever seen his apartment? It's so . . . empty. Like a builder brought in a few pieces of furniture for an open house."

"I've never been there," he admitted, wondering why that was. Tony had been at his house numerous times, and they'd been acquainted since he first moved to Aragon. "But that's not why you called me."

"No. He got fresh, is all."

"What do you mean fresh?"

"He kissed me, and I didn't want to be kissed."

"That's all?"

"Isn't it enough?"

"He never talked about the doll idea?" Rick asked insistently.

"Only to say we'd talk about it 'later.' Can't we go now?"

"Sure." He drove away from the station. "I'm so sorry, Ivy. I never dreamed Tony would get pushy."

"Pushy! He had the totally wrong idea about it. I only went there to talk about a limited edition doll!"

"I know that, and it's my fault."

There was so much contrition in his voice that she wanted to comfort *him*.

"You probably don't know him all that well," she said magnanimously.

"I should have before I let him get anywhere near you."

"You thought he was just a lonely widower. I guess he is. He didn't do anything that terrible, Rick. He let me leave."

"To walk home alone! It's nearly seven miles! He's going to answer to me!"

"No! You've done enough. By coming to get me. Please, Rick, promise me you'll just let it drop."

"He deserves—"

"No! Please."

"I'll pretend it never happened," he said, gritting his teeth, glad that his dentist and doctor each had wives. It was going to be trouble enough changing his accounting firm and taking his checking account to a less-convenient bank.

"We're going to your house?" she asked when he passed Rimrock Road and went down Montoya Boulevard to his street.

"I'll drive you home later. You don't mind, do you?"

"No." She'd never mind spending time with Rick.

He squeezed lemons and oranges to make his favorite summer drink, nonalcoholic and refreshing, insisting that she sit in a living room chair and put her feet up to relax. He carried two tall, cold glasses into the room and sat on the floor beside her.

"No more interfering neighbor," he said sheepishly, resisting an impulse to rest his cheek against her leg.

"I guess you meant well." If only he had the same good intentions about pairing her with the only man she really wanted: him.

"I don't think my motives are very laudable." He'd wanted her to find someone else so he wouldn't feel so responsible for her; now he wasn't sure.

He took her hand, just holding it, saying little. Sitting on the floor, dressed in old tan shorts and a faded red knit shirt, he brought her fingers to his lips, almost absentmindedly kissing her knuckles.

The small gesture affected her so deeply, she wanted to cry. Rick did care about her; he just didn't care enough. The only lesson she'd ever wanted from him was how to win his heart.

He broke the mood abruptly, standing and taking both empty glasses to the kitchen.

"I won't make you climb the fence tonight," he said. "I still owe you some hose."

"No, that debt's been settled."

"Come on, I'll drive you around the long way."

No way was ever long enough for Ivy when she was with Rick. This drive was painfully short, and she knew he'd leave her alone at her door.

"Ivy," he said softly, standing outside her front door, "I can't tell you how sorry I am for getting you into something so unpleasant that you had to walk out."

"You didn't let me walk."

"No, and I'm glad you called me."

"It seemed fair." She tried to joke, but it fell flat.

"Am I forgiven, then?"

"Yes, of course. I'm not angry with you." How could she be after the wonderful, quiet time she'd just spent with him?

"I don't want you to be."

In slow motion he lowered his head, letting his lips make a feathery trail across her forehead.

"Thank you," he whispered, pulling her into his arms for a long, infinitely sweet kiss.

Without parting her lips he ran his tongue along the line where they met, making her tingle with joy. She'd waited too long, and this might be her only chance: one brief moment to provide a memory that would last forever. Letting her instincts take over, she covered his mouth with hers, sucking the long-denied sweetness from his lips and probing with her tongue until they both had to gasp for breath.

Then, breaking away before he reacted, she quickly opened the door, stepped inside, and closed it, reeling from her own audacity and the feverish yearning that had prompted it. Covering her lips with her hand, she wanted to preserve the taste and feel of his mouth for all time.

Rick staggered rather than walked back to his station wagon, astonished by the fervor of Ivy's kiss and rocked by his own response. Not even on the beach, naked in his arms, had she responded with such desire. Who would guess there was a powerful store of passion in such a delicate woman?

He wanted to go back, to feel her writhe in ecstasy under

him while he made her totally his. Clutching the steering wheel, memories of their idyllic night at the beach flooded his mind. He could taste again the salty tang of her breasts and the cherry sweetness of her mouth. If he did go back now he was certain she would deny him nothing; the frenzy of her kiss told him that. He didn't start the car, fighting a Herculean battle with himself.

Finally, engorged and aching, his senses painfully sharp, he drove away, knowing that he was inadequate in the one way that really mattered to Ivy. No matter how wonderful, how fulfilling it would be to sleep entwined with her slender, lovely legs, to awake and feast on her compelling charms, he couldn't wholly satisfy her; he wasn't ready to ask any woman to share his whole life, not now, not when he needed all his energy and concentration to test his commitment to painting.

After a sauna and a cold shower, the relaxing effects of which were soon negated by his undisciplined thoughts, he began in earnest to clear the spacious second-floor room of photographic equipment. Fine weather wouldn't last forever. He needed an indoor studio for serious painting.

The lights were out in the bungalow below his window. He hoped Ivy was sleeping soundly, at peace with herself, but he didn't see how she could be. He didn't drop into bed himself until it was light enough in the studio to work without artificial lighting.

CHAPTER SEVEN

Where was her pride? Ivy wondered glumly, standing in front of the bathroom mirror conscientiously working the bristles of her toothbrush over each tooth. Skinny-dipping was nothing compared to what she'd done last night, practically attacking Rick when he gave her a friendly, neighborly good-night kiss, undoubtedly inspired by a guilty conscience, not passion. She might as well put a big sign in her backyard: IVY LOVES RICK.

He'd sat in his car a long time before driving away; she'd watched him from her dark living room. Her kiss had been as blatant as a placard hung around her neck: available, one lonely female, no strings attached. What man wouldn't give a little thought to that invitation?

Rick had thought about it and left. That could only mean making love on the beach hadn't been the magical experience for him that it had been for her. Of course, how could it have been? He was a photographer. Beautiful, glamorous women filled his life. Nothing anyone could teach her would make Rick fall in love with her.

But now he knew how she felt. That was the terrible part. He wanted her to be sophisticated, and she was a born klutz, wanting to cling to him like ivy on an old brick wall.

Replacing the toothbrush in its holder, she rinsed her mouth, then puffed out her cheeks at the image in the mirror. Making funny faces wasn't sophisticated, either. Maybe she'd take her new look one step further and have her hair shortened just a little more. Did it really matter if Rick didn't care?

Mentally gathering the shattered remnants of her pride around her like a cloak, she decided it did matter. Romance wasn't everything: she had other reasons to be proud of herself. Still under thirty, she had a good income from Karol Ann and a reputation as a top doll designer. She didn't need Rick Winterset or his embarrassing attempts to pawn her off on one of his friends.

When the local stores opened for the day, she made an appointment at Ginger's Head Shop for a new trim. She didn't need Sincerely's fancy salon to look the way she wanted to look.

Even with a lovely sideswept hairstyle, done with as much talent as her last one, Ivy decided she still didn't have the California look. Because of Rick she'd been avoiding her yard, working inside and failing to soak up the golden sunlight. She was too fair to expose herself to midday rays, but if she sunbathed early every morning, she could slowly tan her body. A neighbor's presence shouldn't deprive her of the use of her own yard!

Making a trip to town for groceries, she bought a bottle of tanning lotion, then wandered through a few clothing stores. Midsummer sales were in progress, and she was pleased to find a crisp white halter sun dress in her size, buying it because the backless dress gave her another incentive to get a tan.

The next morning she began her tanning program. It was a glorious day, and in the distance she saw the hills drying to a mottled yellow-brown under a cloudless sky. Covering her plastic exercise mat with a purple- and blue-flowered beach towel, she stretched out on her back in her seldom-worn lilac bikini, setting the timer she used with her kiln to make sure she didn't overdo. By the time she turned over onto her stomach, unfastening her top to tan evenly across her back, she was so sleepy that she forgot to reset the timer.

Rick showered after his early-morning gardening, made a big breakfast of scrambled eggs and toast to hold him well into the afternoon, and went outside to paint. The sight of Ivy stretched out on her stomach on a beach towel with the top of her bikini unhooked surprised him and made him deliriously happy. He checked his emotions, though, knowing that she was angry at him for letting her down. Drawing his lips into a thin, grim line, he tried to get on with his work as though she weren't there, concentrating on the way the light hit the yellow crest of a distant hill, applying paint with his finest sable brush in an attempt to capture the texture of sun-bleached grass.

His hand worked mechanically as his eyes strayed again and again to the provocative length of her body lying immobile on the towel. He imagined rubbing warm, scented oil on her sun-heated flesh, wiggling oily fingers under the narrow strip of cloth stretched over her firm, round buttocks.

To lie so still for so long she had to be asleep. How long had he been struggling with the same grassy slope while his mind darted over the fence? Too long, he realized, worried because Ivy could get a severe burn if she'd fallen asleep accidently. His first instinct was to rush to her side like Sir Galahad, but she wasn't going to appreciate being rescued by him. He walked to the fence, anyway, and softly said her name. When she didn't show any signs of waking, he called more loudly.

"Ivy. Ivy!"

Climbing over the fence, he automatically brushed the powdery whiteness from his jeans and walked over to her, again saying her name. She stirred but didn't wake.

"Ivy, you're going to burn." Stooping beside her, he could see the pink sunburn on her back and shoulders. "Hey, wake up!" He gently touched her upper arm, still pale and soft on the inside.

She awoke feeling just a little dizzy from the sun's direct rays. Starting to sit, she remembered too late that her top was unfastened. Grabbing for the easiest covering, she pulled the towel over her front but not before Rick's eyes rested on the ripe swell of her breasts.

"I'm sorry," she murmured, averting her eyes.

"You should be! Why are you apologizing?" he asked as an afterthought.

When she didn't reply, he continued his rebuke. "You'll end up with skin like old shoe leather if you make a habit of sleeping in the sun."

"I won't!" she snapped. "But thank you for waking me."

"I think you're burned. I should've called you sooner. I didn't know how long you'd been out."

"I set my timer," she said, clutching the towel over her breasts with one hand and reaching for the timer with the other, remembering that she'd been too sleepy to reset it after she'd turned over.

"I didn't hear it. What do you have in the house for sunburn?"

"Nothing, but I don't think I'm burned too badly. Just a little."

"You're too optimistic. You don't know the California sun. I have some ointment that can take the sting out of anything. Go inside and I'll bring it over."

"That's really not necessary," Ivy protested.

He ignored her, leaping the fence and sprinting toward his house, taking the steps to his back entrance two at a time.

Running to my rescue, she thought dejectedly as she fastened her bikini top and gathered the towel, timer, and mat. He probably sets broken birds' wings and wears a Santa Claus suit for the Salvation Army at Christmas time, too. She didn't know how many more good deeds she could stand from him!

He came to her workroom door carrying an opaque white jar with a black lid, unscrewing it and holding it out for her inspection. The yellowish substance could've been face cream or hand balm.

"My pharmacist mixes it for me. An old family formula to take the sting out of burns. I'll put some on your back."

"I'm not sure I'm burned. My back doesn't hurt."

This wasn't really true; she'd put on a blouse over her bathing suit, and the soft, old cotton made her shoulders smart a bit.

"Turn around," he ordered, helping her out of the blouse when she complied.

The cream was cold on her hot flesh, but Rick's fingers caressed her gently, spreading the slightly greasy cream from the tops of her shoulders to the edge of her bikini bottoms. Did she only imagine that he lingered longer than necessary at the end of her tailbone?

"You don't need to do this," she protested halfheartedly. It felt so good to have him massaging her back.

Her face felt hotter than her back, and the discomfort at the backs of her knees was nothing compared to the fluttering sensations she felt in between her legs. Each well-lubricated stroke of Rick's fingers was more unbearable than the last, for reasons that had nothing to do with sunburn.

"Stop, Rick. That's enough."

"I'll leave the jar here with you," he said, but he continued rubbing her shoulders.

"Thank you, but it isn't necessary," she insisted, standing up from the couch.

"Keep it. I have another on hand."

"Well, thank you."

She looked into his face, trying to read what was behind his kind words and solicitous actions. It bothered her that he didn't meet her direct gaze. Was he telling her not to misinterpret his concern? How could he touch her and not feel her body's traitorous response? Couldn't he guess what sweet agony it was for her to be so close to him, desperately hoping for a sign that his interest was more than neighborly?

"I thought I'd have a few people over Saturday night," he

124

said, standing up and stepping away from her just enough to make her suspect that it was a retreat.

"When did you plan this little get-together?" she asked suspiciously.

He shrugged his shoulders, unwilling to admit the idea had just come to him.

"I'll have a few friends from the agency that commissioned the sock ad. Mostly married people. You can make the numbers even for me." He wondered if Ned Linson would be available; being five foot five hadn't killed Ned's social life.

"Sorry, I'm busy," she lied, not knowing whether to be hurt or furious. How could he expect her to be the extra woman in his life, available for odd-numbered parties and unattached friends?

"I should've asked sooner. Are you going somewhere?"

If she was, he wouldn't have to organize a dinner party just to cover his impulsive invitation.

"Yes. I'm not sure where yet."

"I left my painting outside." He gestured toward the yard, frustrated because he couldn't solve his problem with Ivy. Did she have a date on Saturday night? It was none of his business, and he certainly wasn't going to ask. "I'd better get back to it."

He seemed to wilt as he walked through the sun-seared yard and crossed the fence, but she attributed it to the abrupt change in temperature. Maybe her air conditioning was set too low. After an uncomfortable shower that proved she was sunburned, she glanced out the back window to see that Rick had given up on painting. His easel was gone and so was he.

In Minnesota she'd had sisters and friends who had annoyed her by monitoring her meager social life, but at least those people expected her to be home on Saturday evenings. She'd just told Rick a whopper, and all he had to do was look down on her little house from his lofty mansion to

125

learn that she wasn't going anywhere. Somehow she had to find a reason for being away from the house during his dinner party. Mary Alice was the first person she called.

"I'm working four to eleven Saturday and Sunday," her friend said regretfully. "Too bad. There's a new Vietnamese restaurant I'm dying to try. I'm not sure what their specialty is, but a friend had something like egg rolls and chicken with ginger sauce and gave me a good report."

"Maybe next week, then," Ivy suggested, wondering if she'd get as plump as her friend, trying exotic restaurants with her. She had been overweight in junior high, a bad time for a treacherous body to get chunky. Even though she lost all her excess weight in the ninth grade, she'd felt fat all through high school.

"I have a wonderful idea!" Mary Alice said excitedly. "I know you don't like blind dates, but you could do me a tremendous favor and have a good time, too. My cousin is coming on Friday, and my parents have to be at a computer conference in San Francisco all weekend. Thor will just be sitting around their house alone on Saturday night."

"Mary Alice, I don't think—"

"No, just listen. You can go to dinner, drive along the ocean, show him the local sights. He's totally reliable and quite a gentleman. What do you have to lose?"

"I won't take him to Disneyland," she warned sternly.

"No hats with ears, I promise," Mary Alice said, laughing. "And he won't wear overalls and a baseball cap. He's really neat, Ivy. You'll like him. I'm sorry he's my cousin."

"No sales pitch needed. And don't be disappointed if he hates me."

Going out with Mary Alice's cousin meant she wouldn't get caught in the lie she'd told Rick, but what kind of man was named Thor?

"Thor Hallingdal," she said aloud, thinking it sounded a little too ethnic even for her. If she were designing a boy doll to go with her Norwegian girl, would she name him Thor? It bothered her that her new creation still didn't have a name. She liked to imagine a personality for each doll, as if each were her child.

"Gretchen—too German. Heidi—too Swiss. Heather—too Scotch. Ingrid, Helga, Helen, Berta, Betty, Connie," she mumbled aloud, testing the sound of the names and rejecting all of them.

She spent the afternoon sketching costumes representing other countries, not wanting to send her agent a finished doll until plans for a whole line were complete. Rick's ointment did make her sunburn feel better, but his offhand invitation was more aggravating than stinging skin. No doubt he had still another bachelor friend for her to meet.

Thor looked more like a John or a Paul, she decided the instant she opened her front door for him. He was decidedly not Scandinavian in appearance, and the heroic Norse name didn't fit. Of moderate height with medium brown hair, quiet blue eyes, and thin lips set in a smallish jaw, he was neither homely nor handsome. She knew he was twenty-seven—how terrible, her blind dates were getting to be younger than her—but he could've been thirty-seven. His hair was thin because of fineness, not balding, and he had the lean look of a man who never overindulged in anything, not even laughter. He wasn't what she'd expected the cousin of her lively friend to be like.

"It's nice of you to show me around," he said, escorting her out to a dark blue compact.

He was nice; it wasn't fair of her to feel so bored. Never married, he was courteous, clean, hardworking, family-oriented, neat, considerate, and quiet. And if he agreed with her one more time she was going to scream.

"Isn't this delicious?" she asked in the restaurant, forking off a chunk of Bavarian torte that looked sumptuous but lacked any identifiable flavor.

He considered his identical slice of dessert and answered thoughtfully, "Yes, very nice."

127

Mary Alice was one of his favorite relatives, but he worried because nursing was a difficult profession for a woman. Thor also opened doors for Ivy, anticipated her needs, and hung on her opinions, however mundane. They went to an over-rated movie, but not until he checked to be sure she didn't mind getting home after eleven. She liked Thor for Mary Alice's sake, and because there was nothing about him to dislike. He really was a true gentleman. As a gesture of friendship she invited him in for coffee after two hours of watching a Hollywood funny man pursue an ingenue less than half his age.

Ivy told herself they should have their coffee in the work-room; her shelves of dolls would give them something to talk about. It didn't matter to her if Rick happened to look down from his party and see her there with a man he hadn't ma-neuvered into seeing her.

After an afternoon of swimming and working out at his health club, Rick came home, glad that he wasn't having a party that evening. He fixed a chef's salad for dinner—exer-cise always reduced his appetite—and went into the studio to put a final coat of sealant on a landscape. The wall of windows revealed a sky bright with stars, and at the bottom of the slope beyond his garden, Ivy's workroom was fully illuminated. She wasn't alone. Well, he knew she'd had plans for tonight. He approved. A lovely young woman alone in the foothills should spend time with friends. She'd undoubt-edly do a better job of choosing a man than he had done for her. His clumsy attempts at matchmaking still rankled him. Anyone could misjudge a friend, but two duds shattered his confidence in sizing up people.

He applied a sealing medium over a mountain scene he'd sketched when visiting his sister, noticing when Ivy closed the drapes. The guy was wearing a dark suit; that was all Rick could see from this distance, except that he seemed too slender to be the cowboy she'd had there the night he

128

barged in to pick up Casey. Still, the distance could be deceptive.

Why the devil had she closed the curtains? A woman alone took a big risk bringing a strange man into her home. How many women were raped every year in California by men they were dating?

Damn it, if she hadn't closed the drapes, he wouldn't be worried. No neighbor was close enough to hear her scream, and only he could see into that back room before she'd pulled the drapes. He cleaned his brush and turned out the studio lights. Casey was curled up in the security of his sleeping box. It was bedtime.

From his bedroom Rick could tell that the lights were still on in Ivy's workroom. There was a faint outline along the sides of the windows, but he couldn't tell if the guy was still there. Ivy's car was beside the house, but the man's was out of sight on the street, if he hadn't left.

Rick paced, brooding over the view from his bedroom window. Impatient with himself, he got ready for bed, stripping off all his clothes, then dressing again. The streaks of light beside the windows bothered him. A casual date should've left by now.

What the hell! He couldn't charge over there and butt into her affairs, not without a good excuse.

People didn't borrow a cup of sugar at seventeen minutes past midnight. Of course, in case of emergency, Ivy would always be a good neighbor. What emergency? He ruled out illness and injury, and she'd hardly be the one to summon if there was a robbery in the neighborhood. Of course, if he saw someone in his rose garden it would be the natural thing for him to check on her. By telephone. And what excuse could he give for watching the rose garden at this time of night?

Feeling like a jackass but unable to shrug off his uneasiness, he thrust his bare feet into thongs and went to get Casey, cage and all. If he had to make a sudden trip tomorrow, he couldn't leave Casey alone all day, could he? He worked out the details as he gathered the parrot's supplies in a grocery bag.

Setting the cage on the other side of the fence first, he carefully climbed over it, avoiding splinters and nails, wondering why he was going through with such an addle-brained farce. He was beginning to feel battle-weary from his encounters with Ivy.

She answered the door wearing a full-skirted white sun dress, the top only a halter that cradled pert breasts and exposed the golden expanse of her back.

"Sorry to interrupt," he said sheepishly, then realized he'd goofed. How could he know he was interrupting anything?

She turned her back and nodded at a man sitting on the wrought-iron couch holding a coffee cup. Her shoulders, Rick noticed, were peeling. The little blisters and flakes of skin were endearing somehow, in no way detracting from her loveliness in the white dress. He liked it better than any he'd helped her select.

"Rick, this is Thor Hallingdal." She completed the introductions, saying, "My neighbor Rick Winterset and Casey."

"Casey is why I came," Rick said, feeling awkward even if he didn't sound that way. "Something came up suddenly. I'm desperate for a bird-sitter. Just for a day. Tomorrow."

"Is that an Amazon parrot?" Thor asked, walking over to the cage and examining the blinking bird with the intensity of a fellow enthusiast.

"Yes, a Blue-front. I got him from a breeder."

"My mother always kept birds, mostly canaries."

Thor and Rick talked about birds for so long that Ivy offered coffee to both, which they declined. Thor had been a bird-watcher in Wisconsin. He also did birdcalls but didn't want to go through his whole repertoire. She couldn't tell if Rick was as impressed as he seemed. She wished they'd both leave so she could go to bed. Thor left first, thanking her for

130

the pleasant evening. Ivy said to say hello to Mary Alice for her.

"He seems nice," Rick said when she returned to the workroom.

"Nice or safe?" She didn't know why she felt so cross with her neighbor.

"Sorry I interrupted. I'm leaving at dawn."

"You do that a lot."

"Leave at dawn?" He was sitting beside her worktable, his feet hooked on the chair rungs.

"No, ignore my questions."

"What is your question?" he asked with exaggerated innocence.

"Oh, never mind. Is the vet's name in the bag with the food?"

"No, I forgot. It's Zanderman. He's in the phone book. Unlikely that you'll need him. I'll only be gone a day."

"Casey doesn't stay alone for one day?" she asked skeptically.

"Not overnight." He tried to think of someplace he wanted to spend tomorrow night.

"Where will you be? In case of an emergency."

"I'll be getting a motel. Do you want me to call you?"

"No, I guess not."

"Thor seems like a nice guy."

"Yes, you said that."

"He took you out tonight?"

"Dinner, movie," she said listlessly.

"Good." He tried to sound approving. "Men like to take the initiative. Save home-cooked meals for later, much later. What does he do?"

"Computer programming."

"Good future in that field. You look nice tonight. I like that dress."

"I shouldn't have worn it. My shoulders are peeling."

"I hope you didn't point out your faults to Thor."

131

"Rick!" Being angry made her feel awful, but she didn't want to explode at him. Lowering her voice, she said, "If you can't get back by Monday, don't worry. I enjoy having Casey."

"I appreciate it." There was more he wanted to say, but she didn't seem to care about whether he approved of her date. "Where did you meet Thor?"

He kept using Thor's name. Why did that annoy her? Maybe it was the inflection in his voice. The name was unusual, but he thought nothing of photographing a middle-aged woman who called herself Biffy!

"He's a friend's cousin. She's a nurse and had to work tonight, so I entertained him for her. How was your party?"

"It didn't come off," he admitted. "This other thing came up and—"

"Of course. You don't need to explain."

"I wasn't explaining. Just telling you that—"

"Rick, it doesn't matter. I know you're still matchmaking." I just don't know why, she thought miserably.

"You do better without my help," he said, knowing this was true. Thor hadn't even kissed her good-bye, he'd accidentally noticed, wandering into the kitchen with empty coffee cups while she walked him to the door.

"I only went as a favor to my friend."

"Fine. Well, I'm sure he'll call you again." A man would be stupid not to, he thought morosely.

He sounded jealous; she wanted to believe that he was, but common sense intruded. She'd never refused Rick anything; a man didn't see green over a woman he'd rejected.

"It doesn't matter," she said wearily.

"He's a nice guy." He was trying to convince both of them.

"A man who loves birds can't be all bad. I imagine I'll see him again. His cousin Mary Alice is a good friend of mine."

Old Hollingdell, or whatever his name was, probably wanted a wife to wash his socks and cook fancy dinners for

132

his boss and redecorate the kitchen, Rick thought soberly, grunting in reply, catching a whiff of Ivy's gentle fragrance as she followed him to the door. Well, if prospective wives needed recommendations, he could provide one that would make a groom's mouth water. Ivy Gronsted: naive but wise, inexperienced but sensual, plain but beautiful, childish but maddeningly sexy, with perfect breasts that filled his hands and tasted ambrosial to his tongue. . . .

He felt his face go red and turned to leave, hoping Ivy didn't suspect the effect she had on him. Maybe he was having his midlife crisis early, getting hot and flushed and angry and upset for no reason.

"Have a nice trip," she called after him, but her soft words seemed like a mockery.

A nice trip was what he needed. He slumped down on a hard stool in his kitchen until his rear got numb, watching a corny old movie on the only television in his house, a small black and white he used to watch the news when he ate alone. He had a friend, Marla, in San Diego. She was a few years older than him but looked younger and had no romantic illusions. He'd call her in the morning; no, he'd drive there, then phone. Marla wasn't a morning person, but she was very much an all-night person. He went to sleep thinking of a long evening with an old friend; it was what he'd needed for a long time.

The next day he drove to San Diego, checked into a motel, and spent the evening in a piano bar drinking whiskey sours and singing along with a few of the regulars. Driving home the next day he was sorry he hadn't called Marla. He had a hangover for the first time in ten years. Never again would he invent a silly excuse to check on his neighbor in the middle of the night. She was a big girl, and she had better judgment in picking friends than he did.

Casey had been a good bird, Ivy told him. He wasn't all that thrilled to hear it.

133

CHAPTER EIGHT

Ivy's agent wasn't enthusiastic about ethnic dolls.

"I was hoping for something soft and cuddly but distinctive. With a personal angle," Sara Goodwin said, briskly pacing around the workroom as though she expected to find a masterpiece in the clutter of materials.

"A Cabbage Patch doll, you mean," Ivy said wryly.

"Well, every manufacturer is looking for something competitive."

"Little girls are my specialty. Unless you think the market is ready for a little boy doll."

"Not another one right now. Think cuddly. I'll show the Norwegian doll around, but I don't want to get your hopes up. There's no chance it will be another Karol Ann, I'm afraid. Next Christmas should still be good for Karol Ann, though. Does the new doll have a name?"

"Not yet," Ivy said. "Maybe another name that starts with a *K:* Karla, Katherine, Kandy, Katrina, Kristine."

"Kristine," her agent said. "I like that. Or maybe Kristina."

"A whole line of dolls with *K* names?" Ivy asked, not sure whether the idea was silly. "An Irish Kelly, a German Kate, a Spanish Karla."

"Well, it's a suggestion I can take around with the doll."

"Win some, lose some." Ivy wished she could feel so philosophical about Rick.

Her agent's visits were always short. Ivy couldn't remember ever having had coffee with her, but living so close had one big advantage. She could get Sara's reaction without weeks of anxious waiting for a letter or phone call. Minnesota used to seem so remote. Now it seemed like a peaceful haven, a place where people took root, got married, raised families, things Rick had no interest in doing. Or did he? What did she know, except that he wasn't romantically interested in her?

Alone again after her agent's brief visit, she turned back to the thick sheaf of drawings and plans for her ethnic dolls, unwilling to abandon the project in spite of Sara's lukewarm reaction. Dolls could broaden a child's understanding of different people. Concentrating on European costumes, she hadn't taken her idea far enough: the line needed an Oriental, a Black, an American Indian, representatives of the whole world. Really eager for her ethnic dolls to be a success, she went back to work, doing her best to push unhappy thoughts to the back of her mind. It was important to get more sketches to Sara as soon as possible. She'd do a good job showing the doll even if it wasn't her favorite.

After a week of frantic sketching, modeling, firing, researching, cutting, sewing, and deliberating, she was more convinced than ever that American children needed a line of dolls that would broaden their understanding of other cultures. What she had to find now were novel accessories, the little touches that distinguished her creations. Remembering Gretel Ramon and the exotic enameled jewelry she displayed on herself, Ivy wondered if a miniature pendant of enameled copper was feasible for a doll. Could one be produced inexpensively in large quantities? Fired with enthusiasm, she decided to ask Gretel, calling and making an appointment to go to the jeweler's home studio.

Paul wasn't home when she got to the beach house, a relief because he made her uncomfortable. His wife was more than cordial, inviting Ivy to inspect her workshop and showing the jewelry in all stages from the bare copper forms to finished pendants, bracelets, earrings, pins, belts, and other enameled pieces.

"I'll make a few samples for you," Gretel offered, seemingly fascinated by Ivy's project. "The materials aren't too costly. It's the handwork and my designs that make my pieces expensive."

Ivy also ordered custom-designed bracelets for each of her sisters, gifts for their birthdays in the fall, and a pair of earrings for herself.

"If my workroom faced the ocean I'm afraid I'd waste most of my time looking out the windows," she admitted to Gretel.

"My big distraction is sunbathing. Rick keeps warning me my skin will turn to leather, but I can't resist oiling and baking. Oh, there's Josh down on the beach now."

"Does he live here?" Ivy asked, remembering him from the beach party.

"Oh, no, he's managing Paul's condos and living in one as part of his salary. He just borrows our beach. Come say hello. He knows better than to burst in on me in my studio."

"I should be going."

"Nonsense. Josh was asking about you the day after he met you at our party."

Josh's hair was bleached almost as white as his swimming briefs, and his darkly bronzed skin made her hard-won tan look pale.

"You remember Ivy," Gretel said, shading her eyes with one hand against the glare of the sun on the ocean and shifting the top of her bright fuchsia-and-orange sarong with the other.

"Sure. I wondered why you disappeared so soon at the party." He grinned and offered Ivy his hand, hard and warm against hers. "You missed all the fun."

"Sorry. I wish I had stayed." Maybe then she wouldn't have this painful hollow where her heart used to be, remembering what it had meant to make love with Rick.

"There'll be other parties. In fact, I'm going to one Saturday night at one of the condos Paul sold. Why not come with me?"

"You're inviting me?" She bit her lower lip, wondering why she always said something naive.

"Sure. Tell me where you live and I'll pick you up around nine."

"That's a late start." She'd done it again, rushed in to say something dumb.

"Well, how about it?"

She gave him the directions to her house, then left with haste. Why on earth would Josh McNally ask her to a party? Well, he was nice, and there was no reason why she shouldn't go.

Turning off the water, Rick returned to his rose beds, enjoying the rich scent of soaked earth and the morning fragrance of the blooms. Petals dotted the grassy walkways as less hearty flowers drooped in the punishing summer heat. Even this early on Saturday morning he felt trickles of perspiration on his back and legs, bare except for a worn pair of white tennis shorts. Before going inside, he cut the stem of a single Chrysler Imperial, the dewy crimson petals thriving in the blistering sun, carrying it to a jar in the kitchen. After his shower he'd take it to the studio where he was spending almost all his waking hours grappling with the texture and shading of individual roses, experimenting and rejecting, goaded on by his own determination and the soft-voiced question of his little neighbor.

Deliberately working with his eyes averted from the view of her house, he still couldn't help but be aware of her. He knew when her car was gone, and he never failed to notice when she opened the drapes in the morning and shut them at night. She seemed to work as long and hard as he did, often bent over a table or standing beside a bench late at night.

He frowned, stepping into the shower and lathering his arms and shoulders with strongly scented bar soap, wishing he could scrub his mind clean of distractions as easily as he washed his body. Without thinking about it he dried himself and used the damp towel to shine the aquamarine tiles above the tub, wandering out to the hallway to toss it down the laundry chute. The maid, who came three times a week to clean and launder, never had to waste time picking up after him. That was the way he'd organized his life a long time ago; he certainly didn't need a wife to ride herd on him.

Strolling naked into the studio, he savored the freedom of being able to do exactly as he wished in his own home but found the taste of it somewhat bitter. Absolute freedom was a two-faced mistress. He was wholly his own man, but there was no one there to care that he was.

The curtains were open, but the brightness outside made it impossible to see into the cool dimness of her house. He moved halfway across the room, relying on the darkened interior to shield him from observation, wondering why the sight of her ordinary little bungalow drew him time and time again to stare down in brooding perplexity. He felt a familiar stirring in his loins when he thought about his neighbor and hurried to dress in his painting clothes, cutoff jeans, and a T-shirt stained with dabs of paint.

For the past week they hadn't spoken a word. He gave up on Ned Linson and watched with uneasy curiosity to see if Thor made another appearance at her house. The man had to be an absolute idiot not to pursue Ivy, but, of course, she had something to say about it. Maybe she'd discouraged him, turned him down.

Maybe he was being a damn fool, avoiding her after his offer of friendship and help. If she felt lonely she might go out with just anyone to relieve the monotony. Feeling too disgruntled to get the fresh rose from the kitchen, he decided to do some finishing details on his last landscape. He was seriously considering an offer to exhibit a few paintings

138

at his friend's gallery, a trial showing that worried him more than he wanted to admit.

The day passed quickly, and he didn't bother with lunch. By six o'clock he was ravenous, but fixing a meal to eat alone had little appeal. What harm would there be in asking his neighbor out for a quick supper? He picked up the phone before he changed his mind.

"Ivy, this is Rick."

"How are you, Rick?" Her voice was guarded.

"Weak with hunger. Have you eaten?"

"No, but—"

"How about going out for something with the world's worst neighbor?"

"The man who lived in back of my parents kept chickens until the town made him stop."

"What?"

"I mean, he was a worse neighbor than you. All that chicken feed attracted rats."

"Oh, so I'm only the second worst."

"Hardly." She laughed.

The light tinkle of her laughter made him heavyhearted. "About dinner . . ."

"Oh, I'm sorry, Rick. I can't go."

"I just thought we'd run into the café for the Saturday special, Swiss steak or country-fried chicken, all you can eat."

"I'd like to." She struggled to keep her voice casual and unrevealing. "But I have other plans."

"Oh, a date." He tried not to sound disappointed. "I liked Thor. Seems like a good man."

"I'm not going out with Thor."

"Oh? Anyone I know?" This was unlikely, he knew, but he wanted to be sure Davis or VanderVos weren't bothering her.

"Well, actually, yes."

He bit his tongue, refusing to ask who.

"Josh McNally," she volunteered. "I know you don't like him, but he seems nice, and we're going to a party."

"I'm not your father," he said gruffly, his tone voicing his disapproval.

"No, you're certainly not!" He could be so infuriating! He wasn't interested in her; why should he be so concerned about whom she dated?

"He's been married, you know." He felt spiteful and petty for mentioning this, but more than that, he was worried. Ivy wasn't in the same league with that beach bum.

She didn't know about Josh, but hearing it from Rick only made her angrier. "That doesn't mean a thing!"

"You're not going to enjoy any party he takes you to."

"Rick, I don't think you know what I enjoy!"

The phone went dead in his ear, and he felt like smashing something.

"Casey likes Rick, Casey likes Rick."

"Oh, be quiet!" he snapped at the blank-eyed bird, returning him to his cage.

Rick went to the health club and worked out until it closed, then brought home a hamburger and fries in a paper sack, wolfing them down at the kitchen table and watching TV without bothering to turn on any lights. The little house below his was faintly illuminated, the back drapes open, a night-light glowing in the hallway.

Ivy wore her white halter dress, glad that her shoulders had stopped peeling. She was going to have a good time; there was no reason why she shouldn't.

Josh arrived thirty-five minutes late driving a luxurious Aston-Martin Lagonda. Ivy didn't know it was an Aston-Martin Lagonda, all handmade, even the engine, until Josh told her it was part of his divorce settlement. She didn't understand California community property laws, but Josh pointed out that only three Lagondas were made every week and only twenty-four came to the United States every year.

140

"I've never met a doll designer," he said, smiling at her. "Gretel said you've hit it big."

"I wouldn't put it quite that way."

Except for Rick, no man had shown much interest in Karol Ann. Josh had a thousand questions, mostly about how the dolls were marketed and how profitable they were.

The condo was on the second floor of an early-Hollywood-style development, the architecture a cross between a Spanish mission and a Los Angeles warehouse. Iron stairs were tucked away under a narrow arch, and Ivy had to walk ahead of Josh because they were too narrow.

The condo was about the size of the apartment Iris and her husband had shared before they had children. The owner had furnished it with mission oak rockers that slid around on the slippery imitation tile floor covering, which meant that every time a guest sat down in the crowded postage-stamp-size living room, someone else got poked or bumped by a slithering chair.

"Do you live in this building?" Ivy asked softly, accepting a bright pink drink with a withered slice of orange straddling the rim of the glass.

"I wouldn't let my dog live here," he said close to her ear with a sly grin, "if I had a dog. This is one of Paul's economy condos. He still has seven to unload, and I'm not adverse to making a little commission money."

It was the noisiest party she'd ever attended, with music blaring forth from speakers in the kitchen, living room, and one of the two bedrooms. The other guests seemed to be under some compulsion to laugh, dance, or yell. Ivy wondered about the neighbors, but either they were all there or the surrounding condos were empty. She escaped onto a narrow balcony in back, glad it was only the second story because the rail that ran the length of the building looked about as sturdy as aluminum foil.

"Here you are." Josh came up behind her, running his free hand over her bare shoulder and bending to kiss it.

141

"Horrible press in there, I know, but I've made three appointments to show the wretched condos next week. This is the only kind of party where I'm likely to make contact with people who'll go for them."

"Well, I'm glad your business is booming," she said dryly.

"It's a tough way to make a living, not like being your own boss, running your own business. I never thought about royalties on a doll."

"Well, that's how it works sometimes." About the only thing Josh hadn't asked was her annual income. Maybe he was waiting until they knew each other better; say, at midnight.

"You live in a nice area," he said. "Grossly underdeveloped. All that land for so few homes. I think it might be profitable for a builder to buy the whole street and put in family-style condos. You know, a community pool for the kiddies and tennis courts. Not clay. Too much maintenance. Who owns the property west of you?"

"I don't know their names," she said, "but I'm sure nothing's for sale. My house certainly isn't."

"Well, buying up those houses could be a great investment for you."

He insisted on explaining how his uncle's company would handle the development, making sure she understood that he only free-lanced for Paul Ramon. He had a few deals of his own "in the works."

She poured her sticky-sweet drink over the balcony rail, hearing it splat on the parking pavement below while Josh told her how much the houses on her street should sell for.

"You have the key property. The rest could be developed and yours left as is on the end of the street. What year was your house built, do you know?"

"I forget. It's on the deed."

Josh slid his hand under her halter, squeezing her breast while he talked about federal financing for housing. She pushed his hand away, which didn't seem to hurt his feel-

142

ings, and said that it would be a crime to ruin a beautiful community like Aragon, which did annoy him.

"You have to look at it from all sides," he said earnestly. "Think of the opportunity for people who are stuck in L.A. breathing all that polluted air."

"It could be a commuters' paradise," she said, not surprised that he didn't recognize her sarcasm.

The ice in his pitcher of gin and tonic melted before he finished the first glass, but Rick stayed on the patio longer, sipping and staring moodily at the deserted house on the other side of the fence.

He couldn't hear the car traveling fast on Rimrock Road, but he did see a flash of headlights before it stopped in front of Ivy's house. Counting slowly to himself, he watched the seconds flick by on his watch for a minute, then two. He'd give McNally three minutes to leave; no, five.

Some Pygmalion you've turned out to be, he thought with bitter irony, taking her to a party where she met a parasite like McNally.

The five minutes were up, but the house lights didn't go on. Instead he heard voices coming from her yard and realized that the two of them were rounding the corner of her house, walking into the backyard. If he moved they'd see him, and if he stayed still they'd probably spot him, anyway. Furious with himself for caring one way or the other, he shifted uncomfortably, hearing voices without being able to distinguish words.

The couple disappeared, and several long minutes later the car pulled into her drive to reverse direction and speed away. Almost simultaneously the light went on in Ivy's workroom.

"Rick, I know you're there!" she called loudly from the door.

"Tell the neighborhood," he answered in a lower, harsher voice as he stood up.

Ivy walked to the fence and stood with both hands on her hips, seemingly expecting something from him. Ambling toward the wooden barrier, he unintentionally imitated her by planting both hands on his waist.

"I can't believe you're out here," she said angrily.

"It's hot. I couldn't sleep," he half-mumbled.

"Next you'll tell me you were going to sleep outside."

"I used to be a Boy Scout, and it is my yard," he said, amusement tempering his words. "Did you have a nice time?"

"I had a lovely time," she lied with gusto.

"I'll bet." His amusement faded completely. "What were you doing in the backyard?"

"Showing Josh my property."

"He'd love to get his greedy hooks into this neighborhood, but the Delpontos wouldn't leave if an earthquake split their yard in half, and the Sorensons have it written in their will that the place can't be sold to a developer. And everyone else in the neighborhood feels the same way."

"For goodness sake, Rick, you don't need to get up on a soapbox. I love it here. I wouldn't dream of selling."

"If you ever want to, give me first chance to buy," he said.

"I won't want to."

It was sobering to think that Rick might want to buy her out. She turned to go, exhausted after spending several hours with a human cash register.

"I didn't mean I want you to move," he said hastily.

"Good night, Rick."

"Wait." He bounded over the fence, catching up and grabbing her arm. "All I was trying to do was warn you that McNally is a shrewd operator."

"Aren't you going to tell me he made out like a bandit on his divorce? she asked angrily.

"No, I wasn't going to tell you that." He hated it when she sounded so hurt.

144

"I can hear you gloating." She reached her door and slid it open, but his body was in the way when she tried to close it.

"I'm not gloating," he insisted. The last thing he wanted was to make her unhappy.

"Well, I had a nice time tonight. It was fun." She said it emphatically to convince herself. "It's your idea that everyone I meet has to be a marriage prospect. I like my life the way it is."

"Ivy." He slid the door shut and followed her across the room, catching her in his arms before she reached the light switch.

She touched his bare shoulders, which were revealed by the tank top he was wearing, and she could smell the heat of his body and the faint scent of alcohol on his breath. He lifted her against him, pressing his mouth against her parted lips, kissing her deeply. She could tell that he was both angry and hungry, and she couldn't get enough of him, responding with fury and urgency.

"Ivy!" There was despair in his voice, and his hands were in her hair as he breathed in her heady fragrance.

She burrowed her fingers under his tanktop, relishing the feel of his warm skin, the hard muscles of his back. As his hands moved up and down her exposed back, his fingers opening and closing in a sensual massage, he kissed her again, thrusting his tongue into the deepest recesses of her mouth.

Fumbling to open the hook on her halter, he groaned at his failure and held her even closer, parting her legs with his knee and trying again to free the two strips of cloth from their catch, this time succeeding.

Her halter inched downward, caught between their bodies as he kissed her, deeply sighing because it felt so right to have her in his arms again. Taking a deep breath, he cupped her breasts, shuddering with pleasure as the firm, soft mounds nestled against his palms.

Giddy with yearning, she ran her hands under his top with

a sculptor's touch, delighting in the firm swell of muscles on his chest, the bony hardness of his rib cage, and the tickle of body hair between her fingers. She was so right for him, perfectly fitting the contours of his body, drawing strength from him and returning it with passion. She couldn't imagine wanting to be anywhere else on earth but in his arms.

Fool! her mind cried out to him, don't you know this is the way it should be?

He was like a man opening a chest of buried treasure. Knowing that great riches were there wasn't enough; he had to see all of them for himself. Groping for the light switch on the wall behind him, he found it and flooded the room with light.

"You are so beautiful," he murmured, bending to kiss her firm breasts.

Should she say thank you? she wondered. Should she tell him he was the most attractive man she'd ever met? There wasn't an etiquette book for situations like this, and the bright lights made her self-conscious, destroying the romantic intensity of the past moments.

"It's too light," she said weakly, burying her face against his shoulder.

"No, you should never hide in the dark. You're too lovely, Ivy."

His kiss was light, and sweet, but she backed away, awkwardly trying to pull the top of her dress back in place.

"I love your hair." He caught some gold-tipped strands between his fingers, fanning them out across his palm.

"Sincerely's special highlighting," she said in a strangled voice, shaken by his flattering words and wanting to believe that Rick was admiring the real person, Ivy Gronsted. "It's still me underneath."

"What are you talking about?" he asked absentmindedly, too lost in the silkiness of her hair and the downy softness of her skin to take anything else seriously.

"It's still me, spilling pails, saying the wrong things." She

146

squeezed her eyes tightly shut, wishing he would turn the lights out.

"Come here." He led her to the couch, the metal frame loosely covered by cushions, and pulled her down on his lap, again forgetting himself, kissing her face and neck until she felt weak with desire for him.

"The lights are on," she whispered.

"Yes."

"The drapes are open."

"No one can see into your house but me, and I'm here." He kissed her ear, making her shiver with pleasure.

One of her shoes dropped to the floor as he stroked her hip and thigh.

"My shoe."

He felt her stiffening in his arms but didn't want to believe she was anything but the willing, clinging, passionate woman he'd held minutes ago. The cushions shifted as she squirmed, leaving nothing but the metal-slatted frame under one of his legs.

Standing, he pulled her length against his, wondering why he'd ever thought she was anything but beautiful.

"So lovely." He kissed her, finding no resistance this time, wondering how it could possibly be wrong to make love to this enchanting creature.

"Rick." His compliments confused her, and she felt miserably inadequate.

"Let me stay the night, Ivy." He wanted this so badly, he hardly realized the words had been said aloud.

"Why?" she asked bluntly.

He laughed softly, holding her in the circle of his arms with an incredulous smile spreading over his face.

"Because I want you desperately. I want to make love to you."

"I didn't mean, why do you want to stay." She'd never felt at such a loss for the right words. "I meant, why do you want me?"

Some of her pain penetrated his passion-drugged mind, and he held her closer, caressing her back with gentle pats.

"You're lovely, desirable. Isn't that reason enough?"

"For tonight it might be," she said so quietly, he had to strain to hear. "But will you still feel the same way tomorrow?"

"Ivy." He went limp with disappointment, releasing her because for just one instant he hated her for being right.

She read the defeat in his posture and knew he'd leave. She sensed that he'd still stay if she urged him, if she hugged him and used all the wiles that a woman instinctively knew. They could make love in her bed with rosemaling all around them and the scent of roses in the air. She'd ask him to pick a huge bouquet, and they'd scatter the petals on her fresh white sheet and moisten them with the dew of love.

She was so tempted to beg him to stay that she trembled, the bones in her legs turning to gelatin. For a breathless moment she worried about fainting, then called on her last remnants of pride to stiffen her spine and pretend she wanted him to leave.

"It would be better if you left," she said hoarsely.

"I will." He sounded even grimmer than he looked, but he didn't move.

"It's not as if . . ." She shrugged, finishing the thought silently in her mind: It's not as if you love me.

"I want to be your friend, Ivy." He hoped this didn't sound as hollow and foolish and empty as he thought it did.

"Friend?" Her eyes were filling with tears. "I'm not even sure I know what the word *friend* means to you!"

Was it friendly to try to remake her, then throw other men in her path when he was the only one she'd ever loved? His one valuable gift to her was insight. She suddenly knew why her relationships with men always fell apart: because no other man was Rick. She couldn't pretend she'd ever been in love before. Love had its own special pain; to love without

148

being loved in return was the ultimate misery. She started crying, hot, bitter tears that she didn't want him to see.

"A friend," he said gently, "is someone who holds you when nothing seems right."

He took her into his arms with tenderness, feeling scalded by the hot flood of tears against his upper arm. His mind was working like a switchboard that had short-circuited, a meaningless jumble of sparks and flashes accomplishing nothing. The right words were locked in his throat like gold in an impenetrable vault. He'd never felt so helpless in his life.

"I wish you'd go," she said at last, pulling away and averting her face.

He wanted to stay now more than ever, to comfort her and see a smile of peace and contentment on her tear-blotched face, to undo all the harm he'd done since first meeting her. That's what he wanted to do, but he slowly walked to the door and into the night, cursing his own arrogance for thinking he could tamper with another person's life, meddling with Ivy's self-esteem. He walked his small orchard for hours, finally going to bed after giving the roses a predawn soaking.

All he had to have said was "I love you." Men had said it to her before and not meant it. Some threw these three little words around conversationally, as if they only meant "I like you." Noble, upright Rick wouldn't lie to her; he'd break her heart and reduce her to a churning mass of nerves yearning for him with maniacal intensity, but he wouldn't lie.

She closed the drapes and turned out all the lights in the house, unable to bear the possibility of her neighbor staring down on her misery from his lofty perch. Sitting in the dark workroom, she couldn't even look in the direction of his house. She didn't see the solemn figure stalking the rose garden in gloomy solitude.

CHAPTER NINE

Kristina was going to have her chance. Hanging up the phone after a long conversation with her agent, Ivy found it hard to believe the manufacturer's enthusiastic comments that Sara had relayed to her. The same toy company that had marketed Karol Ann was willing to try a six-doll ethnic series that included one each from Africa, Japan, Norway, Ireland, Brazil, and Arabia, half of the designs Ivy had submitted along with the costumed model. The only catch was that they wanted to make them smaller than her completed model to encourage young girls and adult collectors to buy the whole series. Even though they wouldn't appear in the stores until retailers were stocking for the following year's Christmas rush, Ivy was going to be very busy in the coming months preparing models for all six dolls in the size the manufacturer had specified.

The work might help her remember how it felt to be happy. Since last speaking to Rick over a month ago, she got through day after gloomy day on sheer willpower, filling the hours with as much activity as possible but enjoying none of it. Her parents were urging her to come home for a visit, a long stay, before winter started its usual brutal assault in Minnesota. The warm, sunny days in Aragon made it hard to believe that the leaves would soon be turning crimson on the giant maples in her parents' yard, and she might've been homesick for the drastic changes each season brought in Ramsay if her feelings for Rick left any room for other emotions. It was time to forget him, but her love wasn't so easily governed. Not a day passed that she didn't send thousands of wishful glances toward his house, always hoping for a glimpse of him. When she did see him, it brought only pain, but she was addicted to the sight of him. Maybe the only way to free herself was to move, but she was too stubborn to run away.

The announcement came in a richly textured square envelope that suggested a wedding invitation. She opened it and read the engraved card, staring at it for a long time after the message sunk in.

Rick was having his first show of his paintings next week, and she was invited to the gallery Friday evening for a preview and a cocktail party. How did her name get on the list of guests for this exclusive opening? Had some energetic public relations person used a city directory and invited everyone in his neighborhood? She hadn't lived there long enough to be included in an Aragon directory, if the town was large enough to have one. Only Rick could've suggested her name, and she didn't understand his reason for doing it.

Of course, she wouldn't go. Shuffling through the rest of her mail, she found another invitation for the same evening as Rick's opening, this one for a bridal shower for Abby Chisolm, the librarian who'd helped her with several projects and become a good friend. The shower was being held in Aragon, easy to reach. She wouldn't disappoint her friend, and she certainly wouldn't drive twenty miles or more on the freeway to see the paintings of a neighbor who didn't even talk to her anymore.

The day before the gallery party, Rick called her.

"Remember me?" he asked, trying to sound lighthearted.

"Vaguely."

"Did you get the invitation to my showing?"

"Yes. Congratulations. I'm happy for you."

"I've been working frantically the last few weeks," he said.

"Yes, I imagine you have been."

"I'd like very much for you to come. Will you go with me?"

"Rick, I'd like to, but I have other plans."

"You don't have time to go to the gallery first? The party begins at seven."

"I have to be back here at eight. There really wouldn't be time."

"A private showing, then," he said decisively.

"I could come later in the week." Talking to him made her realize how badly she wanted to see his paintings.

"No, I want you to be the first to see. I'll make arrangements with the gallery to take you there at six."

"Rick, that's going to an awful lot of trouble. I promise I'll go when the show opens to the public."

"Humor a temperamental artist," he said. "Let me pick you up at five. I'll bring you home in plenty of time for your other commitment."

"All right, but I'll drive myself. Then you won't have to leave your guests to bring me home."

"I'll stop by at six, then, and you can follow me in your car."

Putting the shower gift, a set of steak knives, in her car ahead of time, she slid it under the seat to make it inconspicuous and went back to the house to wait for Rick, checking the mirror on the inside of her closet door to make sure she looked all right. Her suit was new, a pale cream silk with a deep peach blouse that was ruffled at her throat. With ivory shoes and purse she knew even Rick would admit she looked sophisticated, but underneath it she was more insecure than ever. Beside Rick she'd still be a small-town hick, tongue-tied with the art patrons. She decided she'd leave the gallery before the guests started arriving.

Watching Rick get out of his station wagon and walk toward her front door brought a lump to Ivy's throat. Looking even more trim and handsome than usual in a three-piece silver-gray suit, he smiled when he spotted her at the window. She didn't trust herself to speak to him. How could she say "Hello, Rick" without crying out all the things she felt? Digging her nails into her palms, she slowly approached the door, swinging it open and facing him through the screen.

"Hello." His smile was warm enough to melt a snowman, and he opened the screen door himself, reaching for her hand and squeezing it gently. "You look stunning."

"Thank you." It almost hurt to talk.

"I'll be glad to drive you both ways," he insisted.

"No, that would take you away from your guests. This is your big night."

"Yes."

"I'm ready. Let's go."

"Yes," he said again, but he didn't move, staring at her with an intensity that made her want to hide.

"How long does it take to get to the gallery?" she asked.

"Less than half an hour." He gave his head a sudden shake and stepped aside so she could lock her door. "Traffic will be heavy right now, so I sketched out the directions, in case you lose sight of me. But I'll watch out for you."

"Thank you." How did he know freeway driving made her nervous?

His fingers brushed hers as he handed over the sheet of paper, sending waves of sensation far beyond the point of contact.

"Drive carefully," he warned.

"I will."

"You're sure you won't ride with me?"

"No, really, I can drive."

She could hardly stand still, wanting so much to be in his arms, to feel his hands on her face and his mouth moving over hers.

The gallery was a series of rooms in what had once been a small hotel. The owner rented the rooms on the second and third floors to artists who sold their own works in them. The whole ground level had been renovated to display the work

153

of prominent local painters. Rick's oil paintings were displayed on easels and on the walls of what had once been the lobby, with a long linen-covered table on one side where punch and hors d'oeuvres were being set out for the party.

"Remember, Sanderson Jarvis, the owner, is a good friend of mine," Rick warned, escorting her up steps into the open area carpeted with midnight-blue plush that had a misty, blue-and-gray art deco design. "I'm getting a better showing than my first efforts deserve."

"He must have confidence in you to do all this."

Rick introduced her to the gallery owner, and they stood exchanging pleasantries, but she was dying to look at the paintings.

"How does it look?" Jarvis asked.

"Great, Sandy. Really sensational. Except for the paintings. Some artist nobody knows," Rick said.

His friend laughed, then left, but Ivy scolded him furiously. "You told me never to point out my faults. How dare you put down your paintings."

"I was only—"

"No! No excuses. I'll decide for myself." She stalked off to the nearest easel, recognizing a corner of her own house in an idyllic scene of the foothills, only Rick had covered her bungalow with climbing roses, giving it a romantic picturesqueness the real house lacked.

She moved from painting to painting, so lost in admiration that she was hardly aware of Rick right behind her. They were beautiful, each one having a dreamlike quality that was as elusive as it was haunting. How could he take the everyday things around him and give them such a mysteriously compelling atmosphere? Each landscape had so much to see that she was reluctant to move on to the next, and his small-town scenes had a humorous, whimsical touch that made her smile. Even before she saw the roses, she planned to be his first customer.

The one still life on display showed the pale lavender Lady

154

X's she'd loved so much in his garden, with a few pure white ones for contrast. Instead of arranging them in a vase Rick had painted them as they lay on his wooden counter, freshly cut, waiting to be placed in a cut-glass container in the background. There was a luminous glow to the loose bunch of flowers that told her it was early in the morning; the velvety blooms were still beaded with dew. She could feel the texture and smell the earthy fragrance just by looking at the oil painting, and she marveled at his wisdom in depicting a steel-bladed knife beside the flowers for contrast: the hard with the soft, the man-made with the natural.

"I'm waiting in agony," he said softly, watching her reaction with obvious signs of agitation.

"I don't know what to say." She had to find a tissue because her eyes were getting misty.

"That bad?" His teasing tone didn't disguise his anxiety.

"Oh, no! That wonderful! Rick, you've come so far since doing the paintings I saw in your living room, and they were good. All of these are so marvelous, I just don't know what to say!"

"That means you like them?" A trace of relief crept into his voice.

"I love them all but especially this one." She gestured at the still life.

"Rick," a man beckoned, bearing down on him and giving him only an instant to say to Ivy, "Don't leave yet."

Leaving wasn't what concerned her. She had to see Sanderson Jarvis, finding him in the kitchen area giving instructions to one of the waiters about the table of refreshments.

"Mr. Jarvis, I want to buy the still life, the lavender roses with the knife." She had her checkbook in hand.

The gallery owner looked a little stunned, but he accepted her check, telling her that the painting could be removed after the show.

"You have to promise me one thing," she said urgently. "You absolutely must not tell Rick I bought it."

He nodded sagely; it wasn't the first time a friend or lover had bought a work at an artist's first showing on the stipulation that the transaction be confidential.

"You can count on me not to say a word, Miss Gronsted."

"I appreciate that so much."

People were coming into the gallery for the party, and Rick was surrounded by well-wishers, playing the part of the debonair artist with grace and ease but letting his eyes roam around the lobby-showroom. He smiled when he saw Ivy and broke away from the group.

"I was afraid you'd left."

"No, I was just looking around. He handles nice work here."

"Usually, yes." In spite of his apparent ease, he couldn't get rid of the knot of anxiety in his stomach. "My stuff is a little old-fashioned, you know."

"Oh, no!" she protested vehemently. "Paintings as good as yours don't have to follow trends. Rick, the lavender roses are so beautiful I want to cry."

"Nothing has ever pleased me more than hearing you say that." He laid one hand on her arm and seemed about to say more when a woman with copper hair and a jeweled collar worn over a violet knit suit interrupted him.

"Rick, darling, I'm just flabbergasted. Imagine, you have two magnificent talents, and I never suspected." She took his hand and seemed about to devour it with two scarlet-tipped claws. "I've already decided to buy that bunch of lavender roses. It'll match my bedspread beautifully."

"I'm not sure that one's available, Biffy." He turned to Ivy. "Biffy, this is my neighbor, Ivy Gronsted. Ivy, you've heard of Biffy Rogers."

"Darling, how nice to meet you." One of the lethal-looking hands descended on Ivy's. "Only I'm not Biffy Rogers anymore. I'm Mrs. Charles Wharton, and Charles hates pet names. He's Charles and I'm Beatrice."

156

"Congratulations!" Rick leaned over and kissed her. "I'm really happy for you, Biffy—I mean, Beatrice."

"Rick wanted to put me to work hustling young talent," Biffy said to Ivy with a grin. "He had the right idea about my giving up show business, but I gave him a terrible time in Vegas." She turned to Rick with a winning smile. "Will you forgive me and let me buy a painting, darling?"

"I'll help you pick out the one you should have."

"I have to leave now," Ivy said, glad that she'd acted so quickly to buy the still life. "Nice meeting you, Mrs. Wharton. Thank you for inviting me, Rick."

She didn't give him a chance to detach himself from Biffy and follow her. She left with one small triumph tucked away: the lavender roses were hers to keep forever.

The bridal shower was like any other prenuptial party where only the guest of honor knew everyone. Ivy won a yellow spoon rest shaped like a pig for making the most words out of the engaged couple's names: Abby and Douglas. One of the librarian's friends invited her to a Tupperware party, and the sister of the hostess embarrassed her with overblown praise when she learned that Ivy was the creator of the Karol Ann doll. Unwrapping gifts took forever, because the bride-to-be not only refused to break ribbons, she carefully peeled back each strip of cellophane tape, preserving the gift wrap in near-perfect condition, saving enough to last until her own daughter had a shower, if she ever had a daughter. Ivy's steak knives were one of three sets received with jokes about not being able to afford steak.

She might've enjoyed the shower, anyway, if she hadn't recognized an alien emotion in herself: envy. How she wished that her friends were gathered around trying to make words out of one special pair of names: Ivy and Rick. Now that would be a challenge: irk, icy, icky.

One of the first to leave, she went out to the street where her car was parked under a street lamp and immediately noticed that one tire on her usually reliable little blue compact was pancake-flat. She could try to summon a motor club truck to put on the spare, which might or might not have air in it, or she could beg a ride from another shower guest. Either way she had to return to the hostess's house.

Douglas, the fiancé who'd made an appearance for the last hour of the shower, offered to drive her home. She didn't refuse. Her car could wait until morning.

In his restlessness the sides of the station wagon seemed to be closing in on him, but Rick knew he'd stay in front of Ivy's house until she got home if he had to wait all night. Blast it, what he should've done was tell Sandy ahead of time that the lavender roses weren't for sale. He'd overpriced that one painting so outrageously, it never occurred to him that it would be the first to sell. Biffy wanted it to match her bedspread, but she'd denied being the secret buyer, complaining that someone had bought it out from under her nose. Damn that Jarvis, torturing him by not giving him a chance to buy it back!

The painting should be Ivy's. As soon as Rick saw her reaction he knew that he'd painted it for her. He could do another like it, but it wouldn't be the same. He desperately wished he had it with him now to give to her. As it was, he was willing to wait all night if necessary to tell her he'd intended it to be hers. That was only one of the things he had to explain tonight.

Cramped and impatient, he got out of the car and walked down the road a few hundred yards. Didn't that woman ever spend a quiet evening at home? He knew she did, but tonight of all nights, he resented every second she spent with another man, whoever he was this time.

A noisy foreign car, obviously in dire need of a new muffler, drove past him and stopped in Ivy's drive, staying there only long enough for her to get out. Rick hurried back to her house along the edge of the road. Ivy was waiting for him, standing absolutely still on her front lawn.

"He brought you home early," Rick said a little sheepishly.

"Even my mother didn't wait up for me after I graduated from high school. Why are you here?" She folded her arms across her chest, both indignant and puzzled.

"I have a good reason for wanting to see you." She was making him feel like a meddler, and he didn't like it.

"You always have a good reason. Why, Rick, why?"

"The neighbors will hear you." His voice was a husky whisper.

"I don't care if the world hears! You didn't even speak to me for a month, so what right do you have to check on me now?"

"Maybe we can go inside and talk." He tried not to show his irritation.

"No, Rick. You don't want me, so let me be my own person. I don't need guidance or counseling or advice or monitoring or protecting or—"

"Damn it, stop!" He put his hands on her shoulders, exercising all his self-control not to shake her. "You can take the trouble to hear what I have to say."

"I don't want to. I don't want you interviewing my friends and passing judgment on them. I don't want you popping in and out of my life, making me care when I don't want to. I hate the way you make me feel, and I hate that stupid old fence, and I want you to stay on your side of it!"

"Will you shut up and listen?"

He pulled her closer, grinding his mouth against hers until she started fighting him, pushing him away with both hands.

"I'm not going to be a hit-and-run victim again!" she cried breathlessly.

"Victim! Am I that odious to you? Does a kiss from me make you a victim?"

Her only answer was a retreat. She ran toward her door, but her spiky heels tripped her up. An indentation in the hard-packed ground sent her sprawling on her hands and knees, more humiliated than hurt.

"Ivy!"

"Don't touch me!" she warned urgently.

"Are you hurt? Let me help you!"

"No, Rick. Get away or I'll scream. Very loud."

He backed off with a sign of disgust. "What are you trying to prove?"

"Nothing. I've been able to pick myself up since I started toddling. I don't need a keeper, Rick. I don't want you interfering in my life."

"Is that what I've been doing, interfering?" Not all the bitterness in his voice was directed at her.

"You've been treating me like a ten-year-old!" She felt immature and childish with her knees and palms dusty from the fall.

"Sometimes you deserve it. Did you ever think I might have an important reason to wait for you tonight?"

"Important to you or me?"

"You're shouting! Stop shouting! You'll wake the whole street."

"The people next door are out of town!" She pointed at the closest house. "And I won't shout anymore because I'm going inside. By myself!"

"Have it your way! The one thing I forgot to teach you was manners!"

"Oh, I'm sure I could learn a lot from someone who stalks around my house at night. And I didn't even have a date tonight!"

"I suppose you just happened to pick up that guy in the foreign job. Where is your car?"

"Sitting with a flat tire in front of my friend's house where I went to a bridal shower. My friend's fiancé brought me home." She fumbled furiously in her purse for the ceramic pig spoon rest. "Here's a prize you can have!"

160

She threw it, and he caught it, stuffing it in his jacket pocket without looking at it.

"Can we go inside and talk reasonably?" he asked.

"No, we can't."

She turned to go, afraid of the effect he always had on her. If he touched her, if he kissed her, it would all start again. She'd have to face the agony of knowing that he wanted her but not on any terms agreeable to her.

She fumbled with her key, shaking under the impact of his words.

"Talk to me, Ivy," he insisted angrily.

"No, no, I can't," she said, walking inside and slamming the door.

She stood with her forehead pressed against the door, listening to Rick scatter loose gravel as he drove away. With her pulse racing and her breath coming in irregular spurts, she couldn't think clearly. Not until much later, after a cup of hot chocolate that didn't soothe her and a warm bubble bath that didn't help to relax her, did she wonder why he wanted to talk. Still, the only thing she regretted was not complimenting him again on the excellence of his first show. She didn't want him as a guardian, a teacher, a neighbor, or even a friend, but she was awed by his talent.

The television station signed off with ceremony, playing the national anthem while a flag waved on the screen. Ivy finally went to bed, glad that the next day was a Saturday when she had nothing more important to do than sleep.

The thuds and crackling sounds woke her, but it took a few moments to realize that they weren't part of a colorful dream she'd immediately forgotten. Close enough to be threatening, they sounded like nothing ever heard in this quiet neighborhood. Slipping into clogs and a short yellow satin wrap from her closet, she followed the noise toward the back of the house, ending up at the window of her workroom.

She saw it but didn't believe it. According to the large-faced clock on her wall it wasn't quite seven A.M., but Rick was outside stripped to the waist, wearing only faded jeans and heavy hiking boots, whaling away at the fence with a long-handled ax, furiously knocking off the boards.

The splintery old strips of wood were falling on the ground every which way, and while she stood at the window, he tossed aside the ax and attacked a stubborn end with a crowbar. Already he'd demolished the fence across half the width of her property line, leaving the peeling posts standing.

Running outside, Ivy watched him pick up the ax again and chop through another board, knocking it loose with one blow. His torso was gleaming with perspiration, the hair on his chest matted, and his shoulder muscles rippling with each swing of the ax. He was working so furiously, she was terrified he'd chop his own foot off.

"Rick!" she yelled, not succeeding in getting him to pause.

Running closer, she wanted to throw herself on him and stop his furious assault on the fence. With one powerful blow he buried the head of the ax in a post and warned her off with an angry shout.

"Get back! You'll get hurt!"

"Why are you tearing down the fence? At this ungodly hour?"

"Did I disturb your sleep?" he asked with cutting sarcasm, stepping close with his thumbs hooked in the loops of his jeans.

"You know perfectly well you did!" She surprised even herself with the vehemence of her accusation.

"You wanted to get rid of the fence!"

"I never said that!"

"No?"

He stomped up to her, looking as if he'd like to punch her, his face grimy with wood and paint dust sticking to it. That was all she had time to notice before he kissed her.

He was hot and gritty and his unshaven face prickled hers.

162

There was nothing gentle or sweet about his kiss; he took and demanded more, punishing her mouth with the same fury that had driven him to attack the fence, now in a shambles behind him. This was a different Rick, and she was a little afraid but not so frightened that she didn't return his kiss with desperate longing.

"Now we can talk," he said hoarsely.

"You didn't have to chop down a fence to talk to me!"

He swept her into his arms, carrying her toward his house, up the stairs to the entrance near the kitchen, up the spiral stairs to his studio. When he lowered her to the floor, she tried to pretend his arm hadn't been under her bare bottom.

He was breathing hard, blocking her exit.

"My studio," he said needlessly.

"So I see." She didn't understand why he had brought her there.

"I need a shower. Will you wait here for me?"

"If you hurry."

Left alone, Ivy struggled to make sense out of Rick's tearing down the fence and his carrying her to his house. Except for her tingling lips the whole thing seemed like a dream. Why did Rick want her there? Why had his kiss seemed so different from the other times he'd kissed her? She shook her head, not daring to imagine what his motive might be.

When Rick appeared in the doorway with a red towel wrapped around his hips, she eyed him warily.

"I painted a hundred roses before I got one right," he said, gesturing at the stacks of canvases. "After you saw the painting of the Lady X's at the gallery I wanted to give it to you. Someone bought it behind my back, and Jarvis won't tell me who."

"You wanted to give it to me?" Her voice was filled with wonder. She was deeply touched by his desire to give her the painting that had meant so much to her that she'd bought it herself.

"Yes, but I can't now. I hope you'll choose one of the others instead—if you find one you like."

"I'll love any painting you want to give me," she said, trying to hold back the tears.

"It's your choice," he informed her.

"But why?"

Rick took a deep breath. "Because you mean so much to me."

"So this painting is a friendship gift?" she asked, her voice trembling.

He was standing close to her, and she could see tiny drops of water clinging to the hairs on his chest like miniature pearls waiting to be gathered. She had to look away.

"Friendship has nothing to do with it," he said, putting his hands on her shoulders and brushing his lips against hers. "I'm in love with you, Ivy."

The beauty of his words stunned her. She wanted to believe him. Oh, dear God, how much she wanted to believe him, but questions were thundering in her mind.

"I don't understand. . . . You tried so hard to find someone else for me. . . ."

"Not for you, for me. I thought I'd forget you if you belonged to another man. I'm not proud of myself, darling."

Darling! She hugged his endearment to her heart, but confusion still hovered like fog in her mind. "On the beach," she said hesitantly, "I thought you cared."

"I did, so much that it scared me. Leaving you that night was the hardest thing I've ever done." He gave her a lopsided smile and gently pulled her into his arms.

"Then why did you do it?" She looked up, trying to read his face.

"I couldn't give you what you wanted."

"I want you," she said in a strangled whisper.

"You needed more than I could offer you then—commitment, security, permanence. Maybe I had some belated growing up to do. I know now," he said, taking a deep breath and holding her closer.

"Know what?"

"That I love you and can't live without you."

"Oh, Rick," she murmured.

His kiss was as soft as the brush of a rose petal. She'd never felt so happy in her life. Touching his lips with the tip of one finger, she noticed how tired he looked.

"Haven't you been sleeping well?" she asked, concerned.

"Not at all last night," he admitted.

"Then you belong in bed," she said lightly.

"I wouldn't mind lying down for a while." He touched her throat, tipping her chin up for a long, lazy kiss. "I may need tucking in," he added.

"I might be able to help you there," she said, smiling mischievously.

"What will the neighbors say?" he asked.

"I only have one neighbor who watches what I do."

"That must be a bother."

"Sometimes. Not always."

He watched her with arched brows, wanting her in his arms with a need that staggered him.

"I'll turn down your bed," she offered, slipping past him into his bedroom. The room was spacious, done in sandalwood with black and red accents. Navaho rugs were hung on the walls and scattered on the gleaming floorboards. She slowly turned down the coarsely woven cotton spread. Feeling Rick's eyes on her, she pushed aside doubts about whether she was doing the right thing.

He was standing by the window overlooking her house.

"You have a nice view," she said, going to him.

"Terrific," he said, running his finger down the vee where the front of her robe was loose. But she backed away from him.

"Are you trying to drive me crazy?" He couldn't conceal his amusement. As a temptress she was delightfully shy.

165

"Yes, I think that's what you deserve."

"For waking you up?"

"No."

"For my other crimes?"

"Are you pleading guilty?" She carried the folded spread to a chair.

"I'd have to hear the charges first."

"Neglect." She pretended to pout.

"Guilty."

"Interference."

"That's not logical, Ivy. Neglect and interference have opposite meanings."

"There's more. Destroying property."

"My own property!" he howled in protest, wondering how long he could refrain from scooping her into his arms.

"Disturbing the peace, making all that racket at dawn."

"Well, I'm guilty of that, too, I suppose. What's my sentence?"

"What all naughty boys deserve. Being sent to bed without supper."

"It's still early morning."

"It's a stiff sentence."

"I expected a spanking!"

"Oh, you . . ." She threw a pillow that missed his face and bounced off his shoulder.

He moved quickly, lowering the venetian blinds over both windows, leaving the slats open enough to admit the pleasant morning air.

"How tired are you?" she asked, meeting him at the foot of the bed.

"Very tired of being without you." He searched her face, warmed by the love he saw there. All of his dreams of undressing her fell short of reality when he slipped her robe and nightie off her. She looked more beautiful to him than Botticelli's Venus, and he doubted that his own painterly talent could do justice to the graceful curve of her neck and

166

shoulder where they flowed together, or the sensual swell of her hip, deliciously smooth under his touch. He ached to be joined to her, but this moment was so precious, he wanted it to go on and on.

Did he know what he was doing to her? Ivy wondered as she caught her breath and closed her eyes, content for the moment to enjoy the wonderful feeling of his hands caressing her. Laying her head against his shoulder, she ran her fingers down his side, over the ridge of his hipbone, and to the fuzzy skin on his thigh.

"I don't know why we're standing here," he whispered against her throat, kissing her parted lips and sliding his tongue into her mouth. She inhaled, drawing his tongue deeper, seeing little explosions of light when she closed her eyes. She felt his arousal pressing against her, and just before he lifted her into his arms, she fumbled with the towel at his waist, loosening it until it fell to the floor.

When he lay beside her, she caressed him with a sense of wonder and awe, touching his cheeks and raining small kisses on his lips and throat. Her fingers grew warm as she trailed them over his chest, moistening his nipples with her tongue, parting fine hairs with her breath, exulting in the knowledge of what exquisite torture she was inflicting. She felt weak with excitement and let her hand rove lower and lower until she heard him groan with pleasure. Quickly he locked her in his arms, but when her leg caught under his, he felt like an inexperienced boy, wanting so much to make it good for her that he became awkward. Getting untangled, he bumped her nose with his elbow and felt sick at the thought of hurting her. Her little giggle told him he hadn't.

"I'm sorry," he murmured, kissing the tip of her nose and nibbling her upper lip, thinking about the delicate perfection of her breasts until his mouth sought one and his hand fondled the other.

Wrapping her fingers in his hair, she found herself trembling. Nerves like hot wires sent shock waves to the center of her femininity, and the intensity of her pleasure was close to agony as he suckled the sweetheart tip of her breast.

Aroused to the point of desperation, he'd never felt desire like this before. Ivy was his, and he basked in her trust, taking their intimacy as the gift of her love. Slowly entering her, he felt consumed by tenderness, needing the slow undulations of her hips and her soft moans of pleasure to reassure him that she was wholly his at last.

Rick unleashed in her a greediness for sensation, as exciting as it was unexpected. She couldn't hold him close enough or love him hard enough. She was grasping for something just beyond her reach. His breath was hot on her throat. "Ivy, Ivy," he murmured urgently. Then he lifted her hips and carried her to a shuddering, explosive climax.

Lying beside each other, their hearts throbbing from the pleasure they'd shared, they felt as if they'd just invented love.

CHAPTER TEN

"I never woke up with a man before," Ivy murmured sleepily, nestling in the crook of his arm.

"I'm glad to hear that." He hugged her closer, wishing for a moment that he could bring the same innocence to their relationship.

All the reasons for keeping her out of his life seemed sophomoric. The lonely summer of feverish painting had done much more than mature his style. He knew now that he never wanted to be apart from her again. He loved her so much, he was frightened of losing her.

"I don't know," he said slowly, running his fingers up and down her arm, "how I could have wasted all that time."

"You were busy painting," she said gently.

"You know what I mean! Do you want to hear it again?"

"Again and again and again."

The words came easily now. "I love you, Ivy," he whispered, nuzzling her ear and letting his hands stray.

Why did she get weepy when she was overcome by happiness? She sniffed and closed her lids to hold back the flood, barely managing to whisper, "I love you, too."

They lazily made love, treating the day as a precious gift and exalting the state of being together into a concert of love. She learned what pleasured him, and he tenderly coaxed her to new heights of joy, cherishing her beyond expression.

The afternoon grew warm as they dozed again in each

other's arms, but the wind stirred the blinds and fanned their skin.

"I think we should get married," he said in a husky voice close to her ear.

"To each other, do you mean?" She hoped he couldn't hear her heart pounding with excitement.

"Is there someone else you'd rather marry?" He leaned on one elbow and searched her face, the golden glints in his changeable hazel eyes glowing with admiration.

"I've had enough prospects thrown my way lately," she teased. "I need to sort them out."

"You haven't been seeing McNally, I hope!"

She laughed, banishing his jealousy with a long, deep kiss. He fondled her intimately, brushing his cheek against her breast. His caress became a little squeeze that made her squirm. "How do you feel about it?"

"About what?" she asked, feigning confusion.

"Getting married," he said, scowling with mock ferocity.

"If I get a good offer I'll think it over."

"A formal proposal?"

"At least semiformal."

He knelt beside her on the bed, taking one hand between both of his.

"This goes against my grain," he warned.

"I tremble at the thought of your wrath." She giggled nervously. "Look what you did to the fence."

"I wanted to be sure I could get to your house without being stabbed in the rear by a rusty nail. I don't want any barriers between us."

"Did that really happen?"

"One night when I came over the fence."

"The night you walked backward all the way to the fence!"

"If you don't stop laughing and start paying attention, you're going to miss an historic moment."

She sat and looked into his face.

"Ivy, darling, will you marry me?"

She didn't try to disguise the tears of happiness that ran down her cheeks.

"Don't cry, please." He leaned forward and caught a salty drop on his tongue.

"Does that mean yes?" he asked.

"Oh, yes, yes, yes. I love you so much." She threw her arms around his neck and buried her face in the hollow of his neck.

He kissed away her tears and crooned sweet nothings into her ear.

Barefooted and wearing robes, they fixed an omelet with mushrooms and green peppers and ate it in his den, feeding each other, laughing self-consciously, trying to discover how it felt to be a couple.

"What will we do with my house?" she asked, taking a final bite of toast from his fingers.

"You'll still need a studio, and I like privacy. We'll keep it for your work and as a guest house."

"I'd love to have my family meet you."

"They will. But I don't want to wait long to get married," he warned.

"We'll have the wedding as soon as you like."

"All we need is a pair of witnesses and a man to say the words."

"In a chapel," she added.

"Agreed," he said. "Next week. As soon as we can get a license and make arrangements."

"It can't be too soon." She drew his hand to her lips and kissed each of his knuckles.

"Will you be so agreeable when you're my wife? I was afraid you'd want a thousand guests and an army of bridesmaids."

"All I want is you." She bowed her head over his hand, holding it to her throat.

"I don't know why it took me so long to realize I can't live without you."

171

"You are a little slow. I'll see what day Mary Alice has off next week."

"I'll ask Sandy Jarvis to stand up for me."

At the mention of the gallery owner she smiled secretly. Rick was still in for a surprise or two.

She slept alone in her own bed that night over Rick's mild protest. He'd never seen her room; she wanted it to stay that way until they spent their wedding night there.

They set the date for next Saturday, Mary Alice's day off. On Sunday Ivy and Rick picnicked by the ocean and made love again in the secluded cove, chilled when the wind turned cool but too lost in each other to be bothered by anything.

Monday, after they bought the license, she told him she'd see him at the chapel on Saturday.

"You mean I won't see you until then?" he stormed.

"No, a bride has a lot to do."

"What?"

"Oh, call my family, even though they won't be able to come on such short notice. Make my dress—"

"Wear anything! Everything else is taken care of."

"Please, darling, I really need the time."

"Anticipation makes the heart grow fonder?"

"Something like that," she said, smiling.

"You won't change your mind?"

"No, never!"

"I'll finish ripping out the fence. Digging out the posts will be murder," he said glumly.

"Remember, I'll be watching from the window."

"Am I allowed to wave?"

Even his pout seemed enchanting to her.

"I'll be miserable if you don't. And I won't say no to a dinner invitation."

The research had been done, but the few days before Saturday were scarcely enough time to do all that she planned. For her wedding costume she chose yellow instead

172

of the more traditional red to go with her black skirt, fashioning the new jacket of a bright lemony faille to be worn over a blouse of the finest sheer cotton, white with embroidered gold and blue flowers. A belt of silver links, found only after making dozens of time-consuming calls, held in place an apron of pure white linen and fine Belgian lace. Even on her wedding day a Norwegian girl wore a lovely apron.

Ivy rejected the traditional bridal crown, a flat, cloth-covered headpiece with gilt disks hanging all around the edges, knowing that a glittering array of ornaments didn't suit her. Instead she fashioned a wreath of yellow and white ribbons to wear on her head with narrow satin streamers falling down her back, each ribbon with tiny silk flowers sewn on it. When Rick phoned to ask what kind of bridal bouquet to get, she asked for a nosegay of white and yellow rosebuds, a choice that pleased him.

Again over Rick's protests she arranged for Mary Alice to drive her to the church where the wedding would take place in a small side chapel. Afterward the four of them would have brunch in a private room of the Oceanview Inn: champagne, strawberries, and finger sandwiches.

"It's bad luck to see the bride before the ceremony," she assured her husband-to-be, more nervous than she'd admit to herself.

Maybe when Rick saw her costume there wouldn't be a wedding. She waited for Mary Alice with a grimly set jaw and hands painfully locked together, her stomach tied in knots by anxiety.

What was she doing? She wasn't even sure herself after a week of slave-driving labor on her outfit. Rick thought she was sophisticated now, a woman who could wear a silk suit and go anywhere on his arm. She could play that role, but underneath she was still Ivy Gronsted from Ramsay, Minnesota, steeped in tradition and small-town mores. Unless he saw that in her before they began their married life, she

173

didn't know how they could have a satisfying future together. In her Norwegian costume she looked and felt like her true self.

Five minutes before Mary Alice was due to arrive she was still tempted to change into a regular dress. Gathering up her bouquet, delivered by a florist an hour earlier, she stood in her doorway, waiting for the event that would change her life forever, knowing now why most brides-to-be surrounded themselves with longtime friends and comforting relatives. She'd never felt more alone in her life.

Mary Alice was one of the members of the Norwegian Society who had a traditional costume, a midcalf black skirt with a jaunty red jacket and, of course, a full apron adorned with white embroidery threads and cutwork. Ivy didn't feel quite so alone after seeing her friend in cheerful folk dress.

"You look so beautiful, Ivy!" Mary Alice hugged her, and they both had to blot their eyes before they drove to the church.

Rick was wearing a suit in his favorite sandalwood shade, the texture silky and rich. His shirt was a shade lighter and his tie several shades darker. Beside him, in a conservative brown suit, Sanderson Jarvis was almost invisible to Ivy.

She searched Rick's face and saw mild surprise, but before either approval or disapproval registered, they were standing in front of a minister with steel-gray hair and a beaming smile.

". . . man and wife," he soon concluded.

There hadn't been any surprises in the short service; they'd never even discussed writing their own vows. There were quite a few things they hadn't discussed, Ivy was soon to discover.

His kiss was tender but quick, and then they were leaving. The whole ceremony had seemed like an abbreviated version of the real thing. It hadn't yet sunk in that she was Mrs. Rick Winterset.

"About the brunch," he was saying, seating her in his

familiar station wagon while Mary Alice went with Jarvis in his car, "I asked a few more people."

"Oh?" She was still totally perplexed about his reaction to her Norwegian bridal dress. Did his silence mean disapproval?

"Sandy convinced me that a lot of people would be disappointed if there wasn't some kind of a reception. I talked to Mary Alice, too, and—"

"You talked to Mary Alice instead of me?"

"You were so busy I didn't want to bother you."

"So you got even by making new plans without me?"

"Nothing like that. There'll be as many of your friends there as mine."

"At the Oceanview Inn?"

"No, we ended up needing a bigger place. Sandy volunteered his gallery. He and Mary Alice arranged everything. I'm practically a bystander."

"Do you like my wedding costume?" she asked abruptly.

"It wasn't what I expected."

She squeezed the holder on her wedding bouquet until it threatened to snap off.

"Sit closer," he said.

"You need both hands to drive." She made a production of putting on her seat belt.

"Maybe I do," he said.

To her astonishment the gallery was full when they arrived. The press of people swarmed in front of her, and almost immediately she and her new husband were separated, Rick whisked away by people she didn't know. Somehow Mary Alice had rounded up almost the entire membership of the Norwegian Society, some of the women in full costume, plus Abby, her soon-to-be married friend, her fiancé, Douglas, and several people from her art group. Even Thor was there, inconspicuous in a three-piece navy suit, escorting a frail-looking brunette wearing the transparent braces used to straighten adult teeth.

Eventually Rick made his way back to her, throwing off introductions on either side, escorting her to a table to cut a five-tiered wedding cake with yellow-and-white-frosting roses.

"I got the color right, didn't I?" he asked.

"This is certainly a surprise." She frowned, but before she could say more, Rick was thrusting a chunk of cake against her lips, telling her to smile for the photographer.

The only thing missing was a band; Sandy had orchestra music piped into the lobby, but the guests soon drowned it out as white-jacketed waiters from a catering service kept guests' goblets full of champagne.

Her sisters would love to be here, but Ivy couldn't wait to leave. Who were all these men who kept pumping Rick's hand? Did every woman he'd ever known have to kiss him squarely on the mouth? He kissed her lightly over a glass of champagne, and she was afraid *he'd* get lipstick on *her!*

She didn't want to ask to leave; he'd think she was overly eager to begin their honeymoon. Nothing could be further from the truth. She needed time to absorb this radical change in her life.

"Isn't this a marvelous surprise?" Mary Alice asked, her cheeks rosy and her eyes sparkling. "I really like Sandy. He and I did all the planning. Rick said to do anything we liked and send him the bills. Did you know that Sandy is single? He was married once, but his wife was an actress. It didn't work out with her on the road all the time. I never thought I'd like a man with a bushy mustache, but it doesn't tickle at all."

Sandy claimed Mary Alice's attention, leaving Ivy to wonder how long Rick would want to stay.

It was dusk when they drove up to his house. They were both quiet during the drive; the enormity of what they'd done was beginning to sink in.

"Mrs. Winterset." He offered her his hand, pulling her out of the vehicle.

When he automatically started walking to his door, she dropped behind him.

"What's wrong?" he asked.

"I want to go to my house."

"Darling, I've heard of separate beds and even separate bedrooms, but separate houses are ridiculous."

"You've never seen my bedroom. I thought we could . . ." She shrugged, not knowing quite how to invite her new husband to share her bed.

"A honeymoon cottage?"

"Something like that."

"All right. Let me do a few things here first, then I'll come over. Oh, Sandy had me put something in the back, a painting. Do you want to unwrap it at my house first?"

"No, I'll take it with me."

Feeling betrayed by the gallery owner, she was pretty sure what it was. Rick had to find out sometime, but she wanted to tell him in her own way that she'd bought his painting.

Carrying the canvas and her bouquet, she made her way carefully through the deepening dusk toward her own house, feeling none of the rapture and excitement she'd always imagined she'd feel on her honeymoon. Rick watched until she was inside, then went into his house.

Unwrapping just a tiny corner of the painting, she confirmed that it was the one she'd bought: Rick's lovely lavender roses. Heavyhearted and unsure of whether her quaint wedding garb had embarrassed Rick in front of his many sophisticated friends, she stood the painting against her doll case and went into her room to get ready for her husband.

A quick shower refreshed her but didn't raise her drooping spirits. She put on her new filmy nylon peignoir, the gown under it a caressingly soft tricot that clung to her slightly damp skin. After vigorously brushing her hair she powdered her throat, breasts, and inner thighs and sprayed cologne on her neck, wrists, and the back of her knees. Still alone, she was beginning to worry that her husband of only hours was going to stand her up.

When he did knock on the back door, she answered quickly, so excited to see him that she felt her knees tremble.

"I've been remiss," he said.

"How?"

"I haven't carried my bride over the threshold yet."

He swept her into his arms, taking her outside and in again, letting her feet slide to the floor but keeping her a prisoner in his arms.

"You took so long," she said nervously.

"Did I?"

He was casually dressed in a maroon sweater and navy slacks with loafers, and she could see that his hair was still damp from a shower and his face freshly shaven.

"It seemed that way."

"Good." He kissed her again, then moved away abruptly.

"Would you like something to eat?" She watched him walk to the window and stare out.

"No, thanks."

"Isn't the view nicer without the fence?" she asked, just for something to say.

"I don't want there to be fences between us. Or games." He kept staring at the yard, his hands locked behind his back.

"What do you mean?"

"Your wedding outfit. Why did you wear it?"

"I knew you didn't like it."

He turned to face her. "It's not exactly that I didn't like it. I don't appreciate your reason for wearing it."

"It's traditional Norwegian bridal wear. I am of Norwegian descent," she reminded him.

"I've got some Scots blood in me, but I didn't wear a kilt to our wedding."

"It's not quite the same."

"No, it's not, because you were testing me." He raised his voice, sounding angry now.

She flushed, not completely at ease with her conscience. "That's not why I wore it, not exactly."

"You wore it because of what I said when what's his name, Nate, came to dinner."

"No. I only want you to love me for myself, the way I really am. Not the way you tried to teach me to be."

"Don't you think I love you?" he demanded.

"Yes, but silk suits and streaked hair haven't changed the person I am. I'm not sophisticated like your friends. I am who I am."

"So you wanted me to marry a folksy girl from Minnesota. You little dunce, don't you know that I'm crazy about you just the way you've always been?"

He took her into his arms, kissing her deeply and running his hands over the transparent material of her peignoir. "This is beautiful," he murmured.

"You did the same thing to me, you know." She turned her face aside, still smarting under his partially true accusation.

"What did I do to you?" He wouldn't release her, bending to inhale the fragrance she'd dashed on the side of her throat.

"You gave me a final exam in front of all your friends." She broke free.

"I did what?"

"The surprise reception. It was really my graduation exercise, wasn't it? To see if your creation could stand on her own two feet without any more coaching from you."

"That's the craziest thing I've ever heard!"

"Then why spring all those people on me right after the wedding ceremony?"

"It seemed like a good idea at the time. I thought it would make you happy. I invited as many of your friends as I did mine."

179

"And I showed up looking like the heroine of a folk tale. I embarrassed you."

"Oh, no. You're totally wrong about that. Totally wrong!"

"Am I?"

"Don't you know yet that you can dress in rags and still be the most beautiful woman in the world to me?"

"Oh . . ."

"I love the way you looked. The ribbons woven around your head, streaming down your back, were perfect, the loveliest bridal hat I've ever seen. And your waist looked so tiny under the jacket, I kept wanting to see if I could circle it with my fingers. It was only your reason for wearing it that troubled me."

He spanned her waist now, letting his hands stray over her hips and cup her bottom with inviting little squeezes.

"Kiss me," he ordered.

"Is that a command?"

"Someone in the family has to give the orders," he teased.

"Oh, you think so!" She skirted around him, but he was too fast, cornering her by the doll case. "I've had quite enough of your lessons."

"You think there's nothing else I can teach you?" He moved two steps closer with mock menace.

"Not that I want to learn!"

"We'll see about that!" He lunged toward her, but she bolted out of reach, giggling, her skirts knocking over the still-wrapped canvas leaning on the case.

"We haven't opened the painting Sandy gave us. I thought the silver tray he sent was more than enough for a wedding gift," he said.

"I don't think this is a gift."

"No?" He started pulling off a strip of heavy tape that held the protective cardboard in place, revealing more of the corner that Ivy had seen when she peeked at it. "Wonderful! He managed to buy back my lavender roses. I wanted you to

180

have this so much that I told him to offer the buyer double his money."

"Rick, Sandy didn't buy back that painting."

"No?" He gave her a puzzled frown but turned the package around to pull tape from the back. "This has your name and address on it."

"Well, yes, it does," she said uncomfortably.

"Which means . . ." He hastily ripped off the rest of the wrapping.

"That I was the one who bought it," she said meekly.

"You bought it? You paid that much money for it?"

"I would've paid anything to have it, darling."

"Why didn't you tell me?" He set the painting on a table and moved toward her, head lowered, hands on hips, reminding her of a bull about to charge.

"The subject just didn't seem to come up," she explained feebly.

"Ivy!" He kept advancing, following her backward retreat down the hallway.

"I wanted to surprise you," she said.

"I am surprised. I've been bothering Sandy night and day about it. No wonder he kept giving me those smug little excuses."

"Some friend. He promised me he wouldn't tell who bought it."

"Some friend is right!" He backed her into the kitchen, cornering her against the refrigerator.

"You wanted me to have it," she said.

"I wanted to give it to you."

"I don't quite understand about California's community property law, but isn't half of everything I have yours now?"

"Something like that, I suppose." He trapped her between his arms, pressing his palms against the fridge.

"Then half of the painting is yours, anyway, so you can give me your half, then it will be all mine again and still be a gift from you."

181

He shook his head and grinned. "I'll never have enough nerve to face reasoning like that in a divorce court."

"Does that mean you're stuck with me?" She touched his sweater, pleased by the softness of the cashmere.

"Hopelessly stuck." He kissed her slowly, opening and closing his mouth over hers.

"You don't really mind about my wedding costume?"

"I haven't been so amused since Casey scared off an encyclopedia salesman."

"Casey! He's all alone!"

"He's a grown-up. I fed and watered him before I came here."

"You mean he can stay alone all night?"

"Of course. What trouble can a caged parrot get into?"

"So the second time you brought him here it was just an excuse to check on me?"

He groaned. "I should've bedded you right away like any smart groom. We don't have to talk about everything tonight."

"Did you really take a trip?"

"I drove to a motel just to cover my silly excuse for checking on you."

"You cared even then!" She flung her arms around his neck and hugged him.

"I loved you. I was just too stubborn to admit it to myself."

"Oh, darling, I feel as if I've always loved you."

"Do you have a bedroom in this place?" he murmured, pressing his face into her hair.

"Um, with a double bed. I like lots of room when I sleep."

"If you really want separate bedrooms . . ."

"Don't tease me anymore," she protested, squeezing his cheeks.

"Never?"

"No, just right now. Come see my room." She pulled him by the hand to her bedroom door.

"This isn't how I thought our wedding night would be," she teased, taking his hand and holding it against her breast.

"You probably didn't expect a nervous groom."

"You, Rick?" she said, loving the faint laugh lines by his eyes and the dark wispiness of his lashes.

"I've never been a husband before."

"I've never been a wife."

"That sort of makes us even, huh?"

"Right on the starting line," she whispered.

"Kiss me."

"Orders, orders, orders." She brushed his lips lightly with hers. "You're not sorry you're married?"

"Never. I'm only sorry I can't be a perfect husband for you."

"You are."

"Convince me." He untied the bow under her breasts, sliding the filmy peignoir from her shoulders.

"So many layers and each one more beautiful," he said softly, inching the long gown over her thighs. He nibbled at her mouth, letting his tongue slide around the inside of her lips, unhurriedly savoring all that a kiss could be.

His skin under the sweater felt feverishly warm, and she left him for an instant, opening wide the single louvered window, letting cool, sea-scoured air wash over her body, turning back to watch as Rick stripped off his sweater, shoes, socks, and slacks, stepping toward her in low cotton briefs, a black band between muscular thighs and his flat, tanned stomach.

Watching her with his feet spread apart and arms at his sides, he smiled wickedly, his eyes glazed with passion and his breath coming in deep inhalations. Standing only inches from him, she gathered her gown on both sides and slowly worked it upward until, clasped in her hands high above her head, it made a veil to cover her face and nothing else.

"In some ancient societies," he said hoarsely, "a bride didn't reveal her face until the marriage was finalized."

"Imagine, marrying someone you've never seen," she said, still holding the gown over her face.

"Quite a surprise."

"A shock."

"How often do we really see another person?" he asked softly, fingering the edge of the gown.

"As often as we want to."

"I want to see you, darling." He gently removed the gown from her grasp, stepping back to admire her with awe. "There was never anything I could do to make you more beautiful."

"If I'm beautiful it's your love that's made me that way." She reached for him, slowly sliding the briefs down his fine, firm legs.

"Then you'll always be beautiful, because I'll always love you."

He held her close, their noses and chins touching, her breasts flattened against his chest. A gentle probing against her groin made her shiver with anticipation, and she wasn't afraid to let him know all that she felt.

"You were right," he whispered, looking down on her with hooded eyes.

"About what?"

"Staying apart. Every night without you was like a session on the rack, but wanting you makes me a different person, a better man."

"Darling." She buried her face against him, hugging him with all her wiry strength.

"No tears?"

"None at all."

She met his mouth with breathless eagerness, hungrily returning his kisses until her lips were tender and swollen, hardly aware of it when he brought her to the bed and wrapped his legs around her, engulfing her in love.

Like a tornado that springs forth from an utterly still landscape, their lovemaking was explosive and frantic. He forgot all the techniques of love, tossing away artifice like confetti scattered by a windstorm, possessing her with primitive abandon and intoxicating love.

She was part of it, crying aloud and reveling in the wild frenzy, losing her self-consciousness as a separate person until the rhythm of their bodies was like the beating of her heart, the lifeblood of her existence, the essence of her being.

Later he bent over her, tracing a rosemaling design of his own over her glistening torso and limbs, planting kisses instead of roses on imaginary vines.

"I'd like to paint you," he said hoarsely, stretching out her arm to receive his paintless artistry.

"My portrait?" She wiggled when he extended a branch to a ticklish spot on her rib.

"No, your body. With a sable brush. Silver rosemaling on golden flesh. A pink bud on your breast and a crimson rose on your thigh."

"I want us to do something we've never done before and will never do again, so tonight won't be like any other night in our lives," Ivy said solemnly.

"It hasn't been like any other night in my life."

"But you'll love me again and again, night after night, won't you?"

"You know the answer to that." He kissed her chin, surprised when she got up and went to the doorway.

"Don't get dressed. Just come with me."

"Barefooted?" he asked in mock dismay.

"Bare-everything." She padded naked into the kitchen.

"I like your wiggle." He pulled her against him, wondering for the millionth time why he'd denied himself the wonder of this splendid creature for so many long, cruel months instead of admitting the truth: he loved her more than enough to give up his meaningless freedom.

"Here, take my roasting pan," she said, thrusting a cold

metal pan into his arms and locating a small paring knife from the drawer.

"What are we going to do?"

"Gather the last rose of summer."

"Roses aren't a one-season flower in California. Shouldn't we get dressed?"

"You said no one can see into my yard but you, and you're here."

He tried to hide the grin breaking across his face, following her through the workroom and across her yard.

"Watch your feet. I may have missed a few nails when I raked," he warned, gingerly crossing the prickly, dry lawn and the rough indentation where the fence had stood.

"We're charmed tonight. Nothing can hurt us."

"Not even spiders?" he teased devilishly.

"They wouldn't dare crawl across our toes on our wedding night."

He looked around, satisfied that no brightly lit windows overlooked their nocturnal errand. Still ahead of him, Ivy looked like a woodland sprite fluttering through the night in naked splendor. He wanted to make love to her on his lawn furniture, but her sense of purpose made him bide his time.

"Here," she said.

She bent and cut a pale bloom, one of the few left in a bed of white and yellow roses. Watching her snip flower after flower and lay each one carefully in the pan he was carrying, he thought of warning her about thorns but knew she was right; the evening was enchanted. There would never be another moment in time quite like this.

Her breasts fell forward when she leaned over a bush, and he wanted to hold her and love her. Still she clipped the roses, pausing only to press a velvety bloom to her nose and inhale its spicy fragrance.

When the pan was filled to overflowing, she smiled with deep satisfaction and led the way back to her little bungalow.

He expected to fill vase after vase with the roses, every

186

shade that was still blooming, but Ivy had another idea. Finding a lovely cut-glass fruit bowl, another of her grandmother's treasures, she started plucking the petals from every flower, mixing them into a rainbow of colors in the transparent dish. Not until the last stem was stripped and the dish overflowed did he carry it back to her bedroom.

Leaving only the creamy-white bottom sheet and two pillows on the bed, she started scattering the petals, dotting the whole expanse with delicate wisps of color, sitting on one side and inviting Rick to do the same across from her.

With the bowl between them they sent showers of petals over each other, laughing as the rose petals caught in their hair and fluttered over their shoulders. When the bowl was empty, the air was heavy with the fragrance of roses. Ivy laid back in the precious petals, ending up in her beloved husband's arms, trembling with desire.

"Can I give you one more thing you'll never forget?" he whispered, brushing a lavender petal from her cheek.

"One more and one more and one more," she murmured, blissfully losing herself in his kiss.

All-new

*Candlelight
Newsletter*

**An exceptional,
free offer awaits readers
of Dell's incomparable Candlelight Ecstasy and Supreme Romances.**

Subscribe to our all-new CANDLELIGHT NEWSLETTER and you will receive—at absolutely no cost to you—exciting, exclusive information about today's finest romance novels and novelists. You'll be part of a select group to receive sneak previews of upcoming Candlelight Romances, well in advance of publication.

You'll also go behind the scenes to "meet" our Ecstasy and Supreme authors, learning firsthand where they get their ideas and how they made it to the top. News of author appearances and events will be detailed, as well. And contributions from the Candlelight editor will give you the inside scoop on how she makes her decisions about what to publish—and how *you* can try your hand at writing an Ecstasy or Supreme.

You'll find all this and more in Dell's CANDLELIGHT NEWSLETTER. And best of all, *it costs you nothing.* That's right! It's Dell's way of thanking our loyal Candlelight readers and of adding another dimension to your reading enjoyment.

Just fill out the coupon below, return it to us, and look forward to receiving the first of many CANDLELIGHT NEWSLETTERS—overflowing with the kind of excitement that only enhances our romances!

Dell DELL READERS SERVICE-Dept. B676E
P.O. BOX 1000, PINE BROOK, N.J. 07058

Name_____

Address_____

City_____

State_____Zip_____